anyth...

Mighty Mighty MONSTERS

SCIENCE FAIR
NIGHTMARE

STONE ARCH BOOKS
a capstone imprint

Mighty Mighty Monsters are published by
Stone Arch Books, A Capstone Imprint
1710 Roe Crest Drive
North Mankato, Minnesota 56003
www.capstonepub.com

Cataloging-in-Publication Data is available
at the Library of Congress website.

ISBN: 978-1-4342-3891-7 (library binding)
ISBN: 978-1-4342-4226-6 (paperback)
ISBN: 978-1-4342-4649-3 (eBook)

Summary: It's time for the Transylmania
Science Fair! Each of the Mighty, Mighty
Monsters have their eyes on the grand
prize, but no one wants to share. With
each monster hoping to snatch up the
winnings for themselves, lines are drawn
and friends become foes. Will the spirit of
competition win out, or will the green-eyed
monster break up the gang forever?

Printed in the United States of America in
Stevens Point, Wisconsin.
012013
007152R

Mighty Mighty MONSTERS

SCIENCE FAIR NIGHTMARE

created by
Sean O'Reilly

illustrated by
Arcana Studio

In a strange corner of the world known as Transylmania . . .

Legendary monsters were born.

WELCOME TO TRANSYLMANIA

But long before their frightful fame, these classic creatures faced fears of their own.

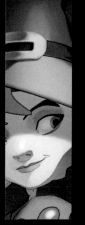

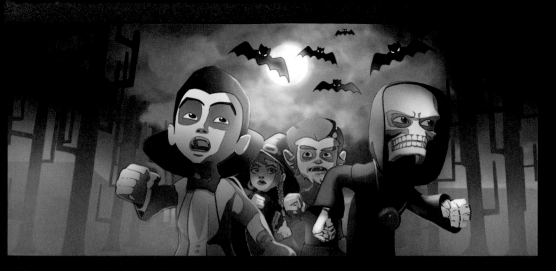

To take on terrifying teachers and homework horrors, they formed the most fearsome friendship on Earth . . .

Mighty Mighty MONSTERS

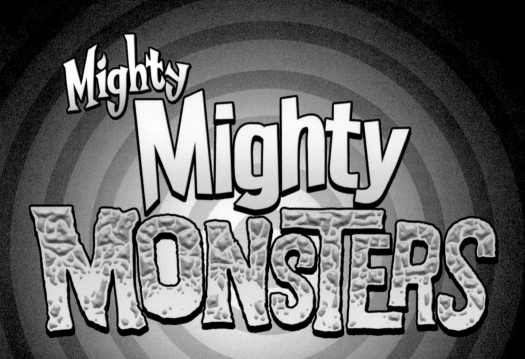

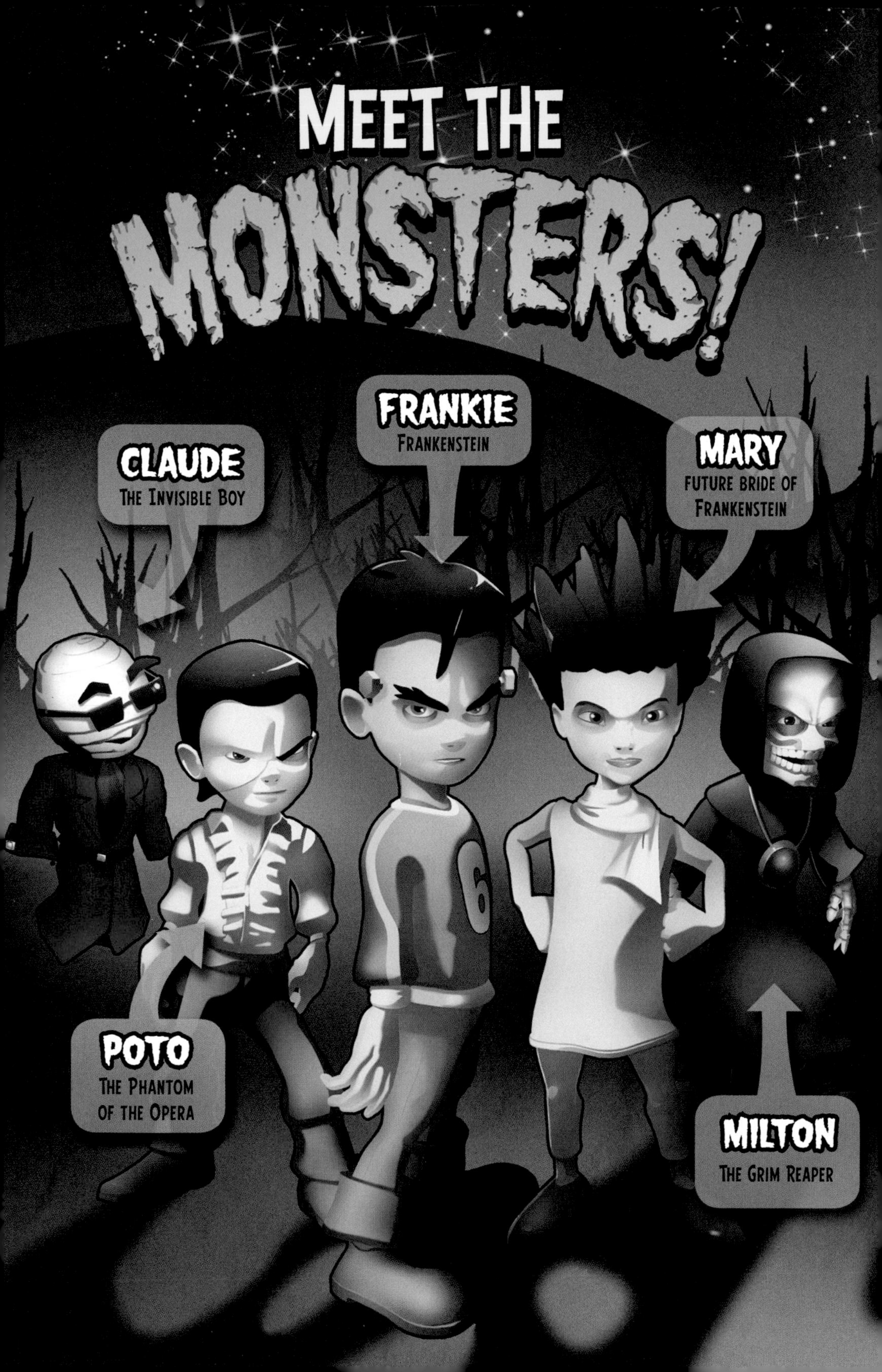
MEET THE
MONSTERS!
CLAUDE
THE INVISIBLE BOY
FRANKIE
FRANKENSTEIN
MARY
FUTURE BRIDE OF FRANKENSTEIN
POTO
THE PHANTOM OF THE OPERA
MILTON
THE GRIM REAPER

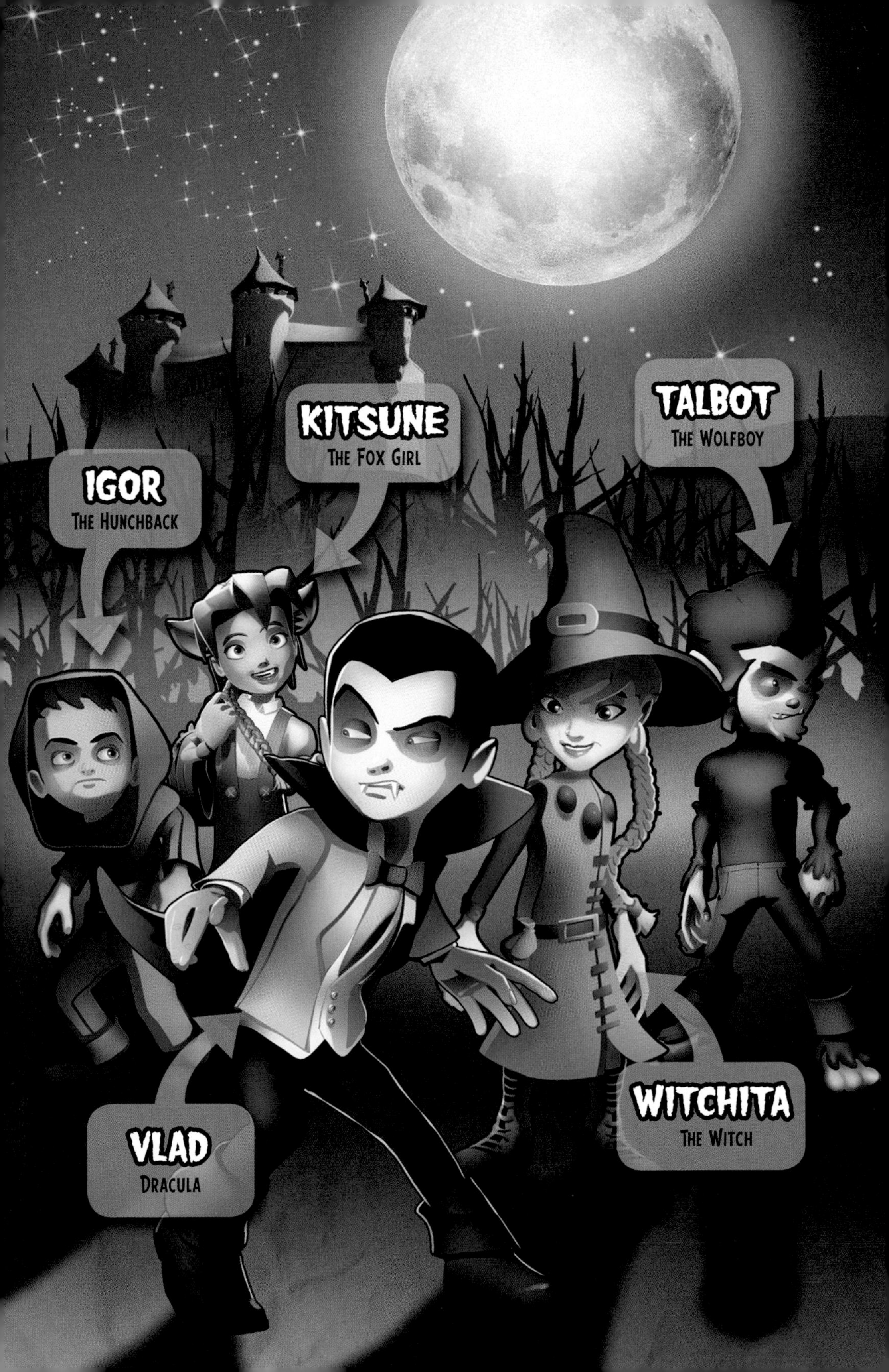
KITSUNE
THE FOX GIRL
TALBOT
THE WOLFBOY
IGOR
THE HUNCHBACK
VLAD
DRACULA
WITCHITA
THE WITCH

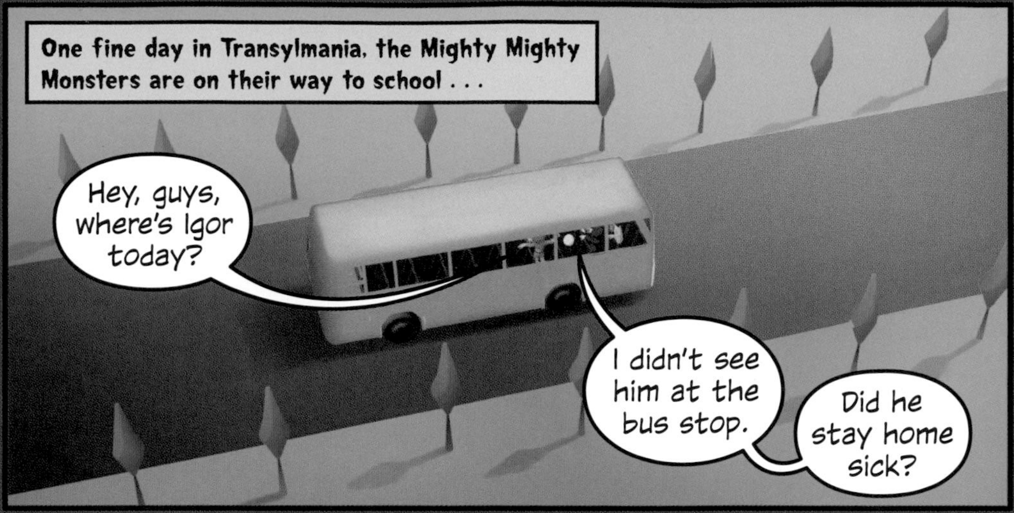
One fine day in Transylmania, the Mighty Mighty Monsters are on their way to school . . .
Hey, guys, where's Igor today?
I didn't see him at the bus stop.
Did he stay home sick?

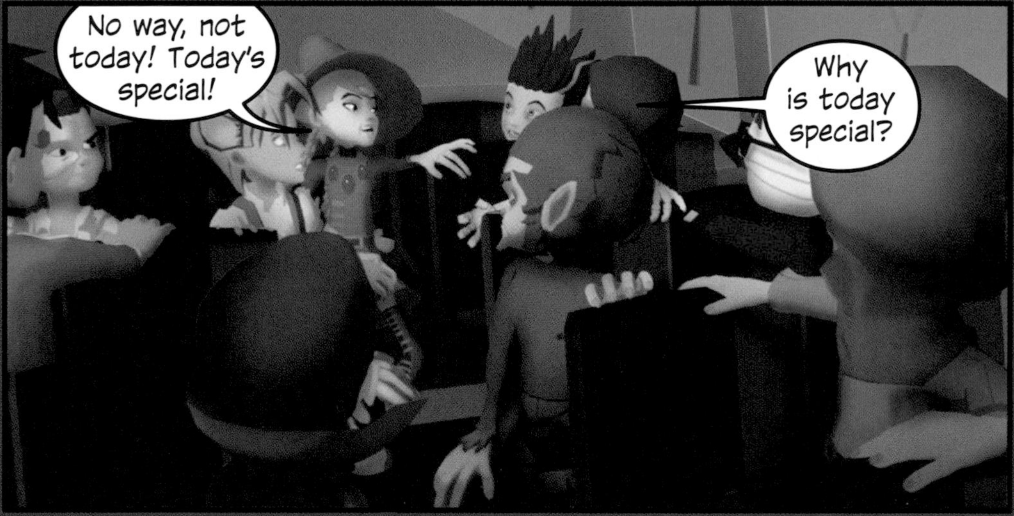
No way, not today! Today's special!
Why is today special?

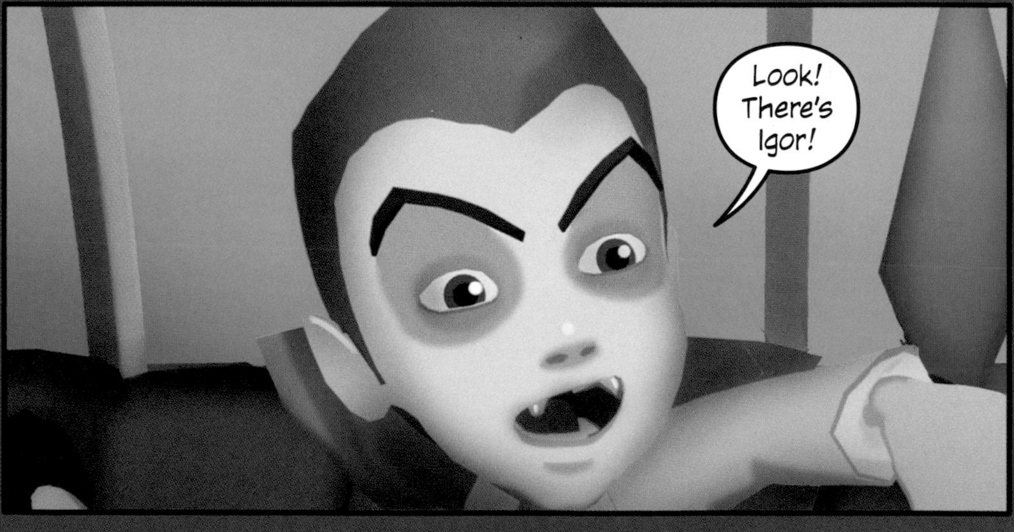
Look! There's Igor!

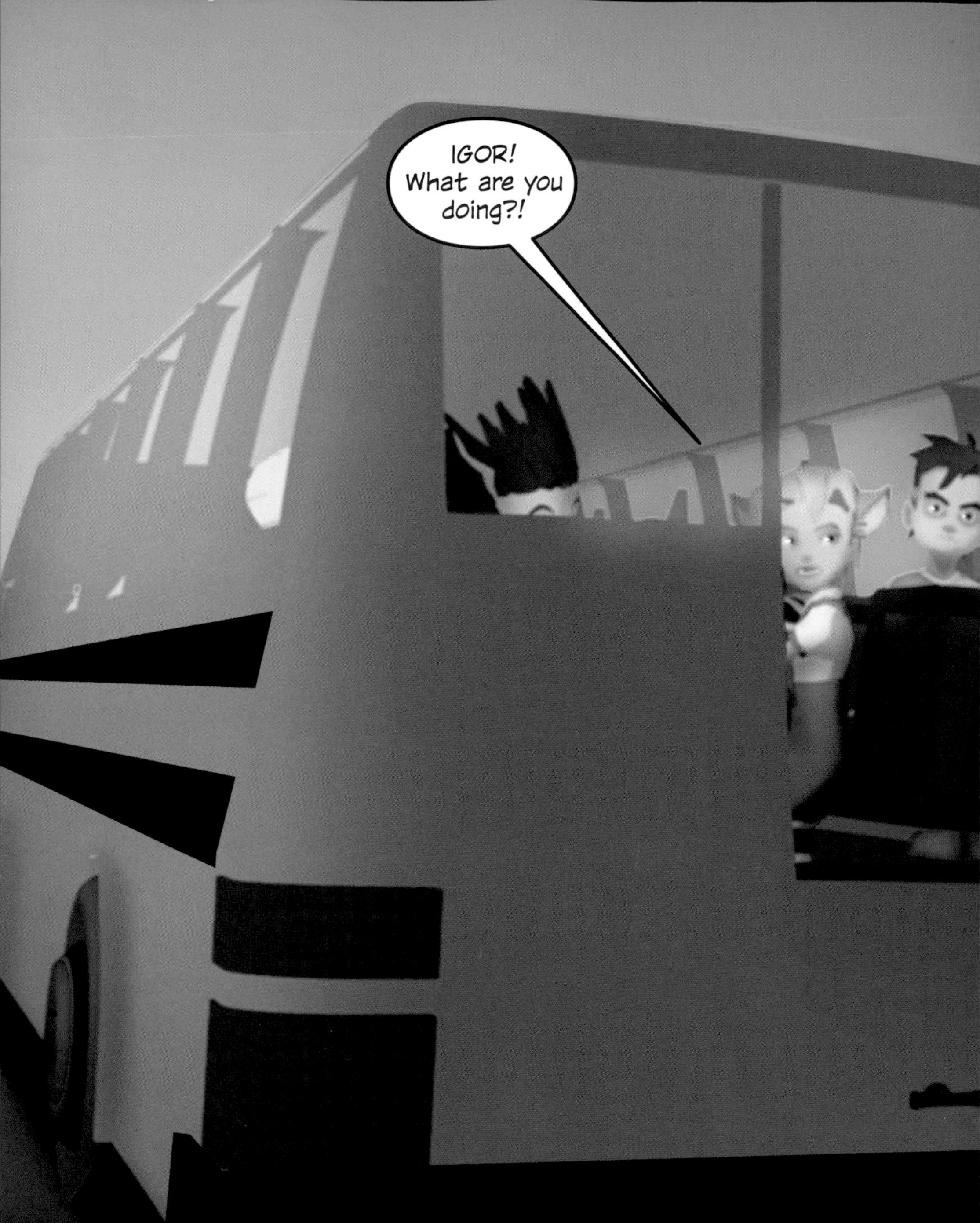
IGOR! What are you doing?!

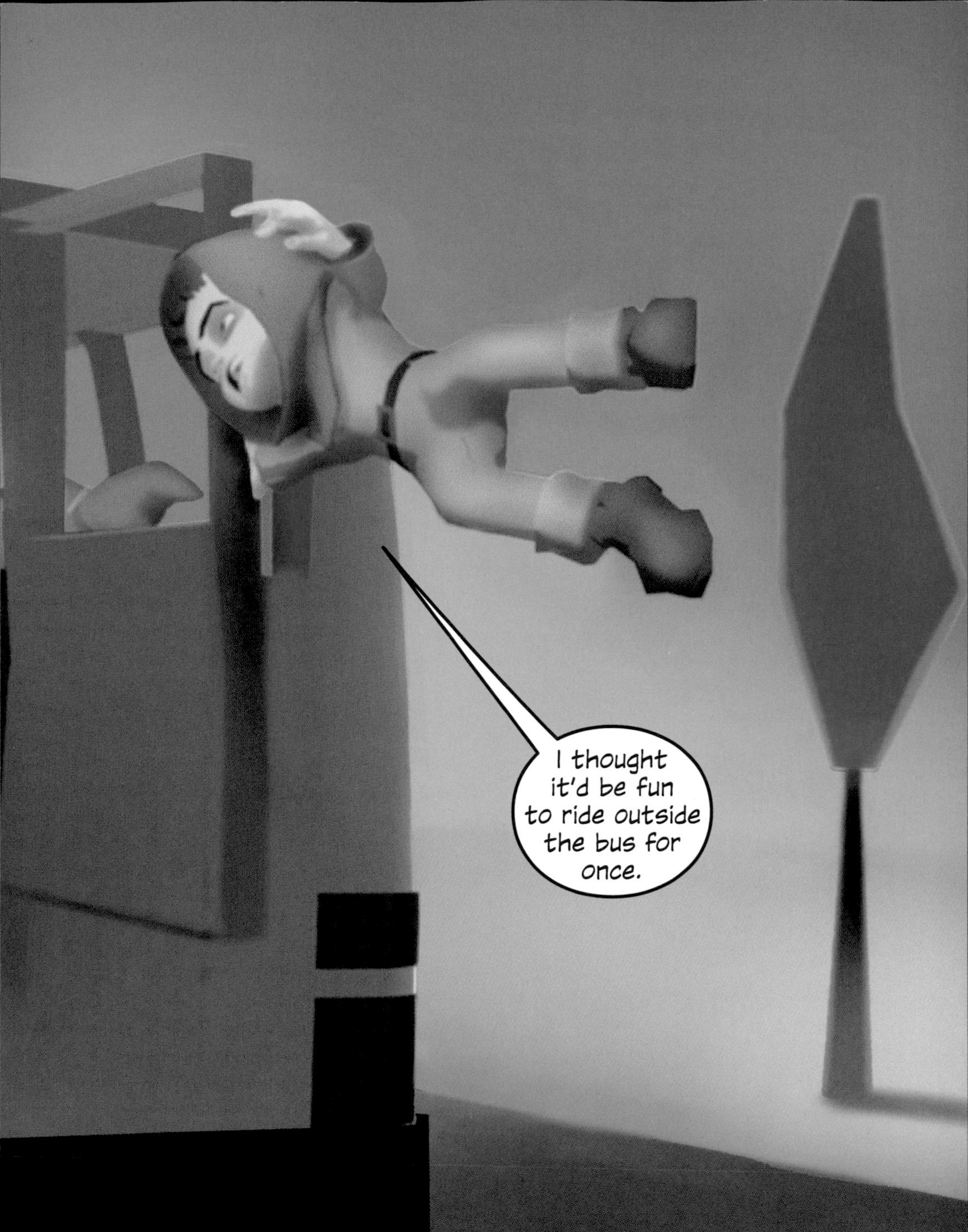
I thought it'd be fun to ride outside the bus for once.

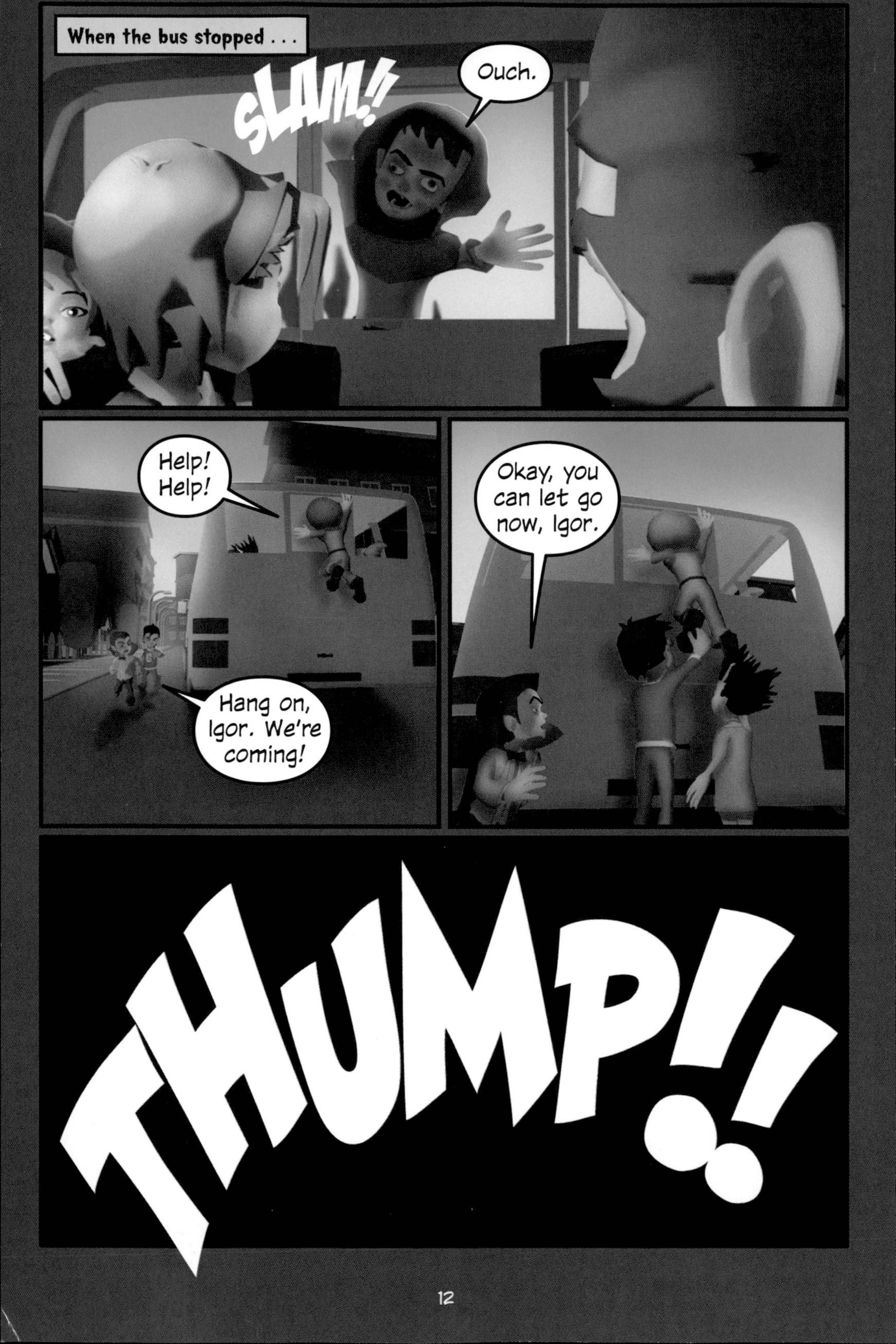
When the bus stopped . . .
SLAM!!
Ouch.
Help! Help!
Hang on, Igor. We're coming!
Okay, you can let go now, Igor.
THUMP!!

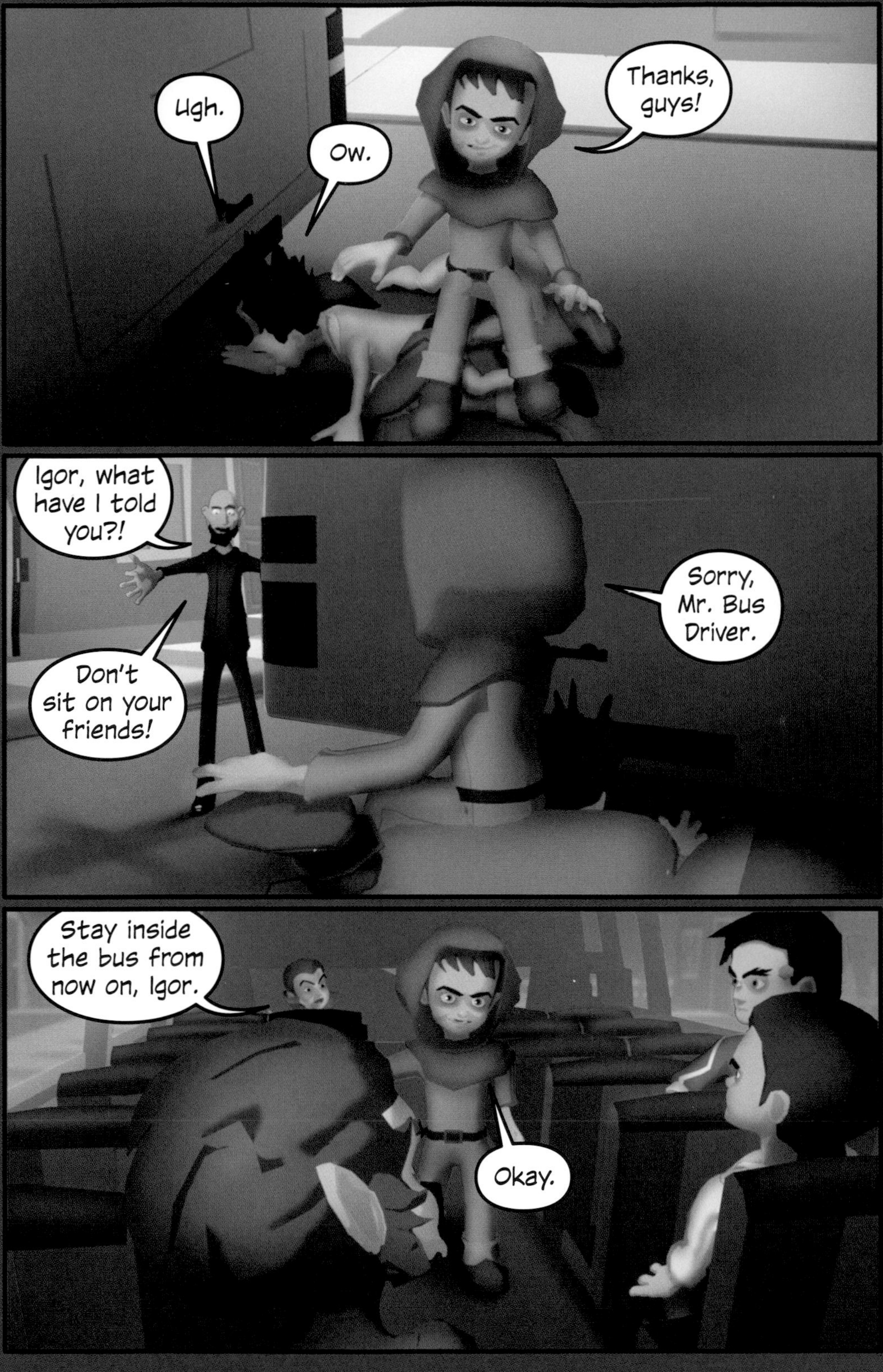
Ugh.
Ow.
Thanks, guys!
Igor, what have I told you?!
Sorry, Mr. Bus Driver.
Don't sit on your friends!
Stay inside the bus from now on, Igor.
Okay.

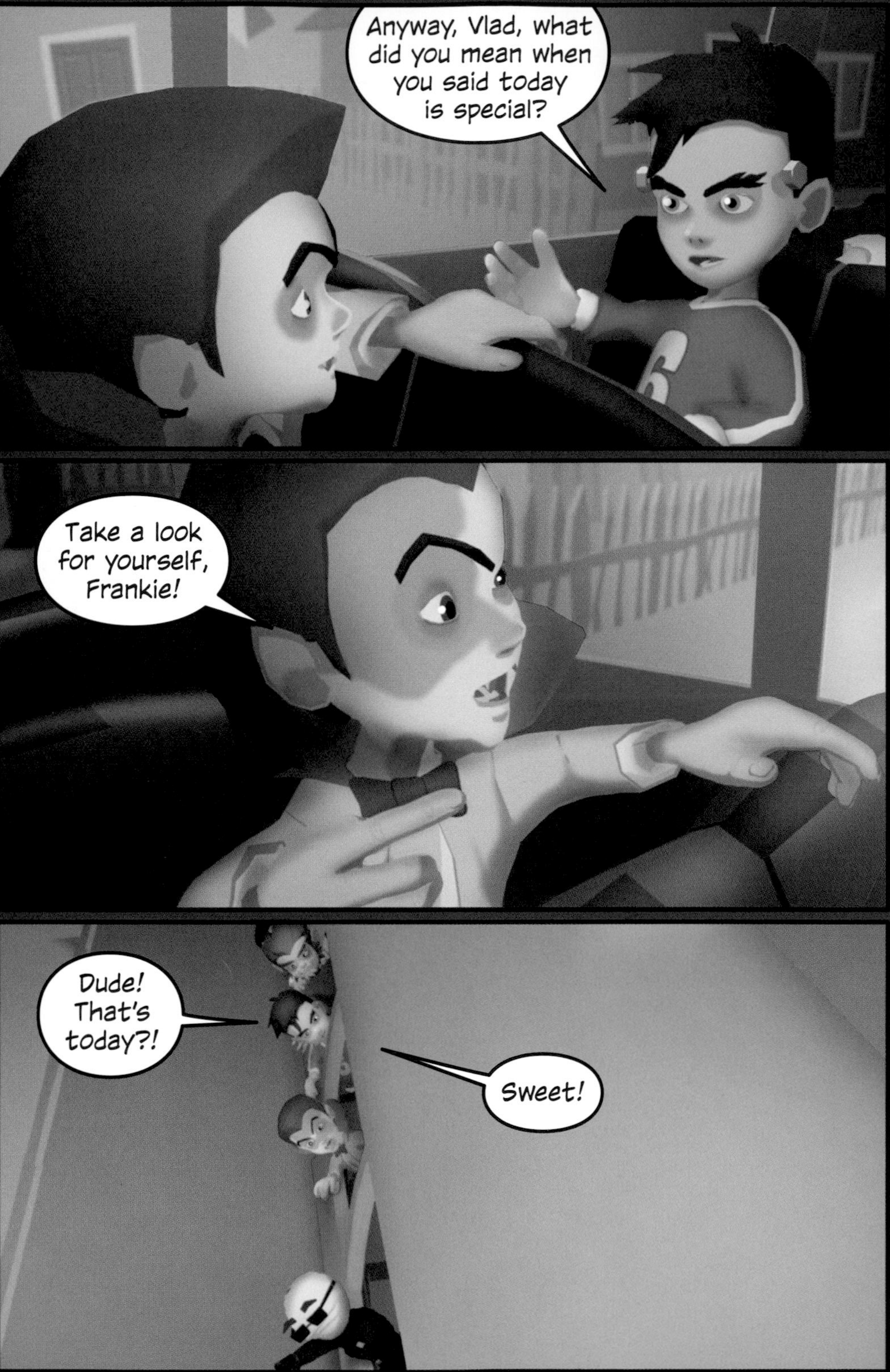
Anyway, Vlad, what did you mean when you said today is special?
Take a look for yourself, Frankie!
Dude! That's today?!
Sweet!

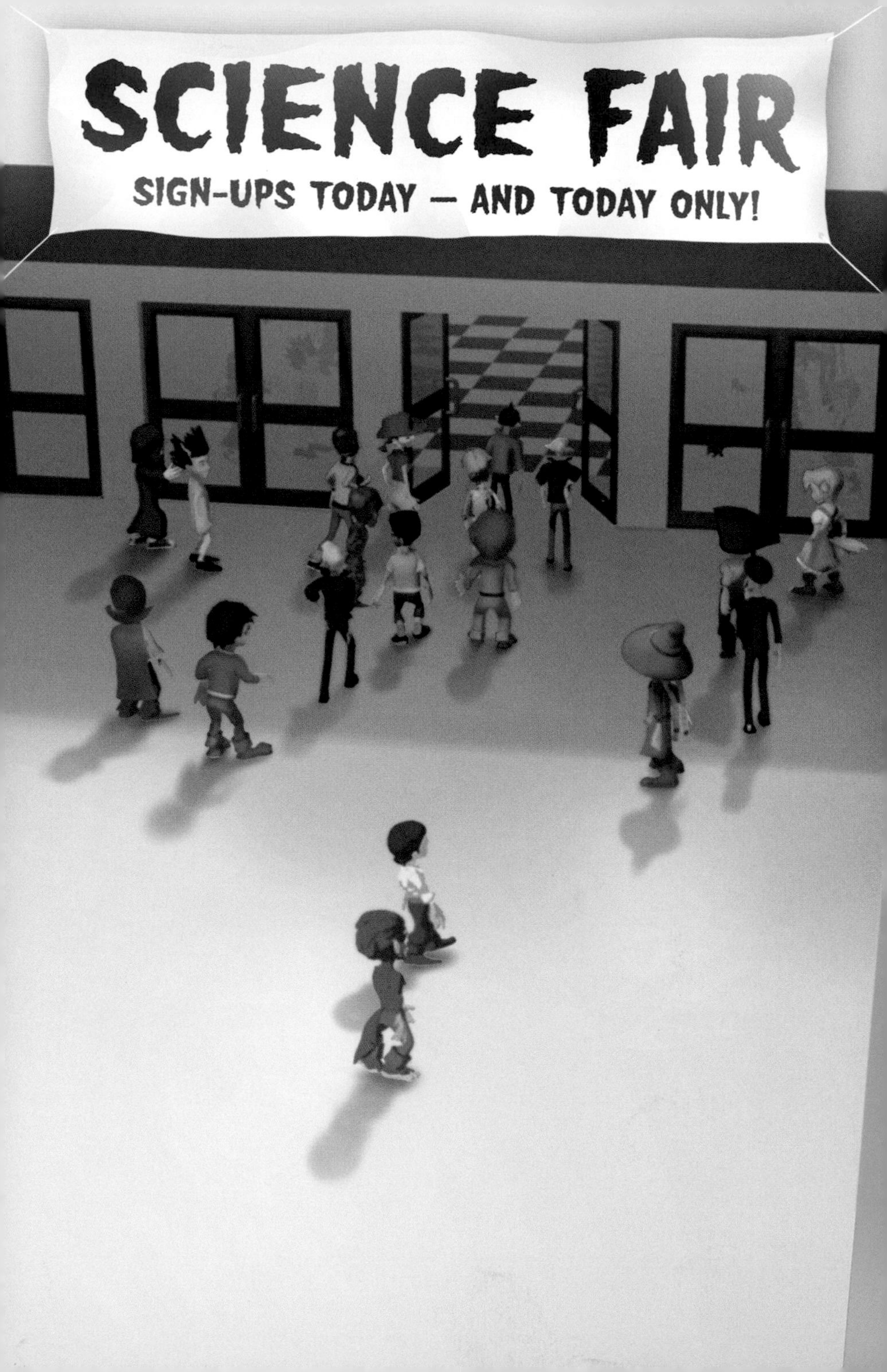
SCIENCE FAIR
SIGN-UPS TODAY — AND TODAY ONLY!

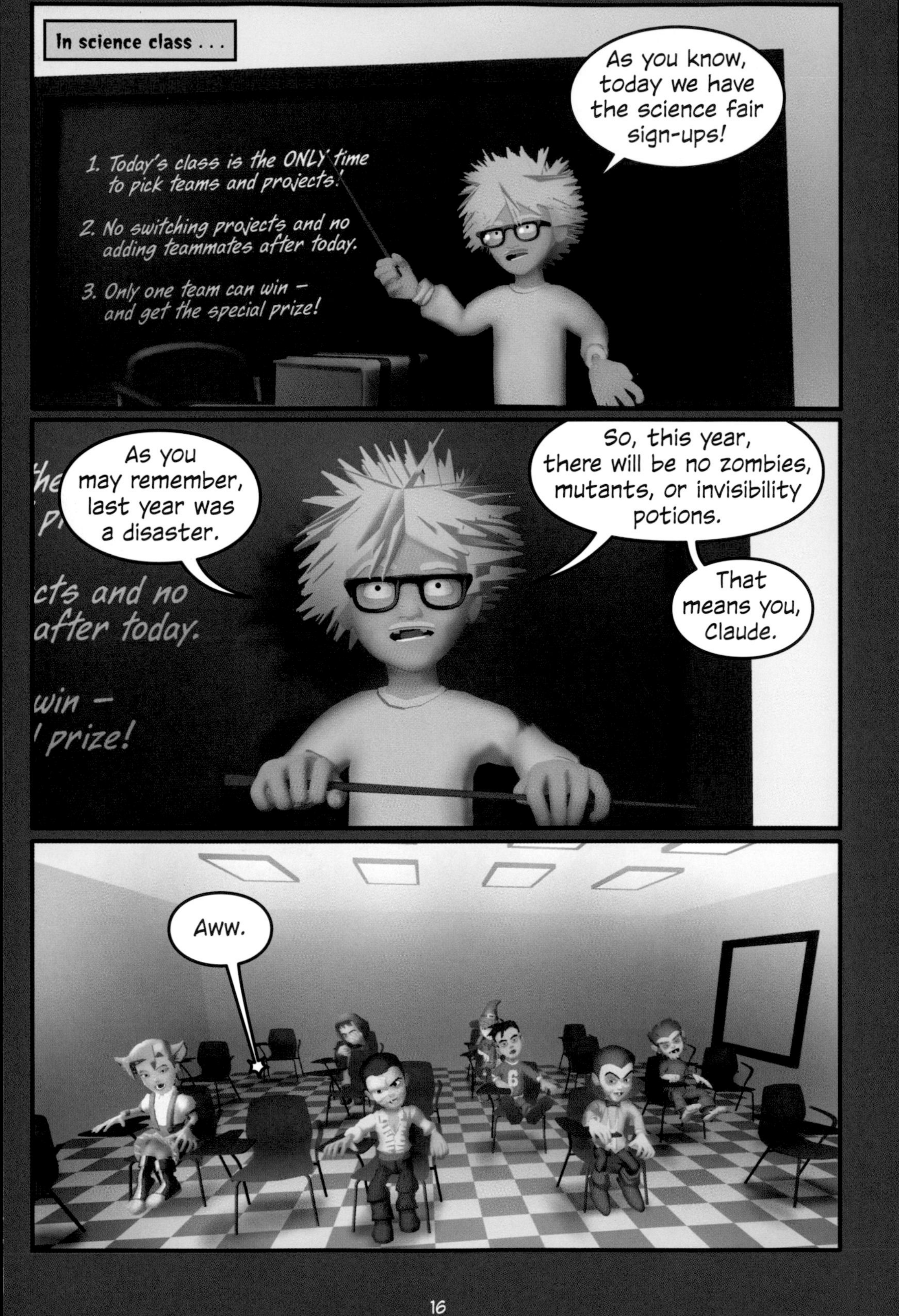
In science class . . .
1. Today's class is the ONLY time to pick teams and projects!
2. No switching projects and no adding teammates after today.
3. Only one team can win – and get the special prize!
As you know, today we have the science fair sign-ups!
As you may remember, last year was a disaster.
So, this year, there will be no zombies, mutants, or invisibility potions.
That means you, Claude.
Aww.

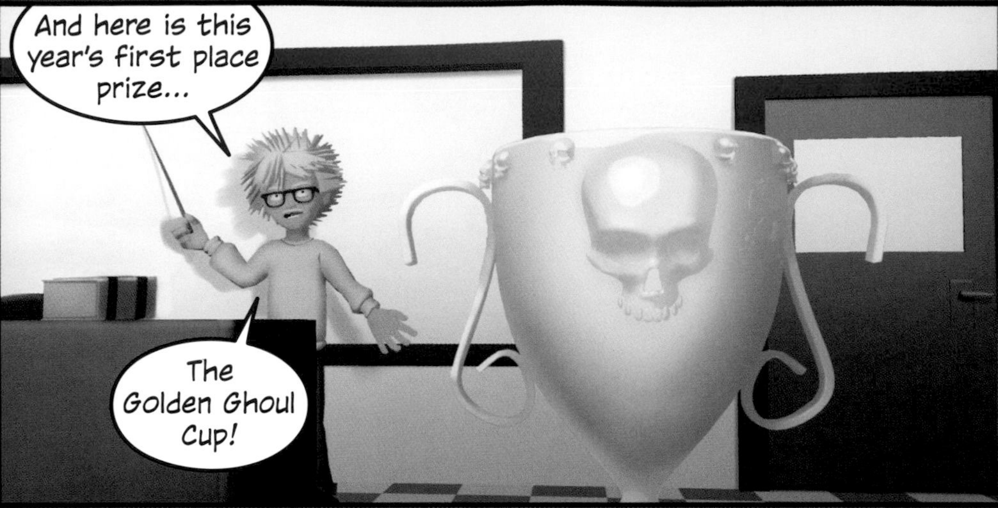
And here is this year's first place prize...
The Golden Ghoul Cup!

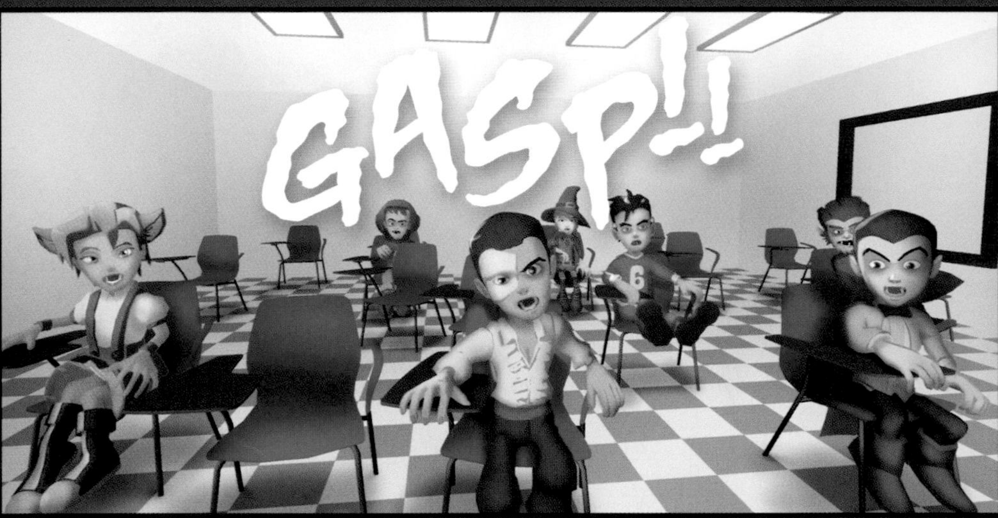
GASP!-!

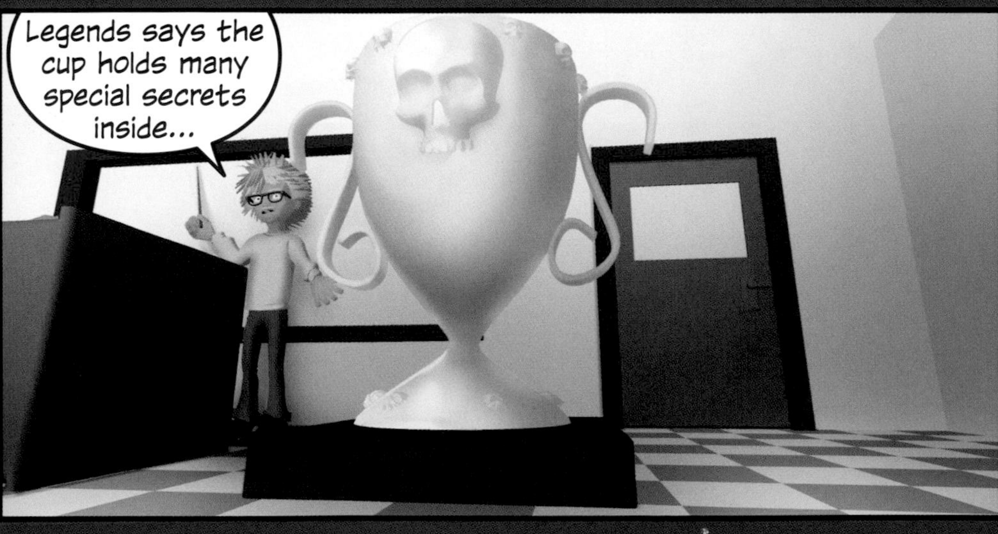
Legends says the cup holds many special secrets inside...

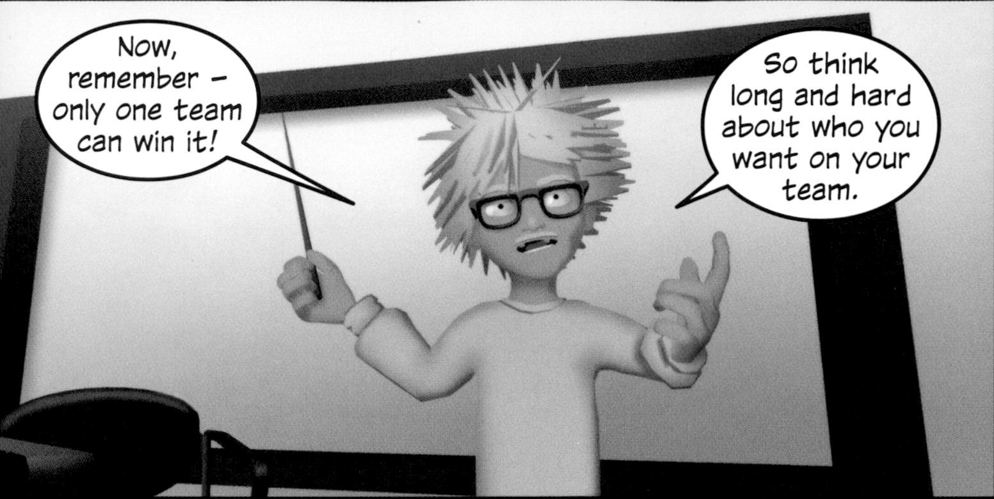
Now, remember – only one team can win it!
So think long and hard about who you want on your team.

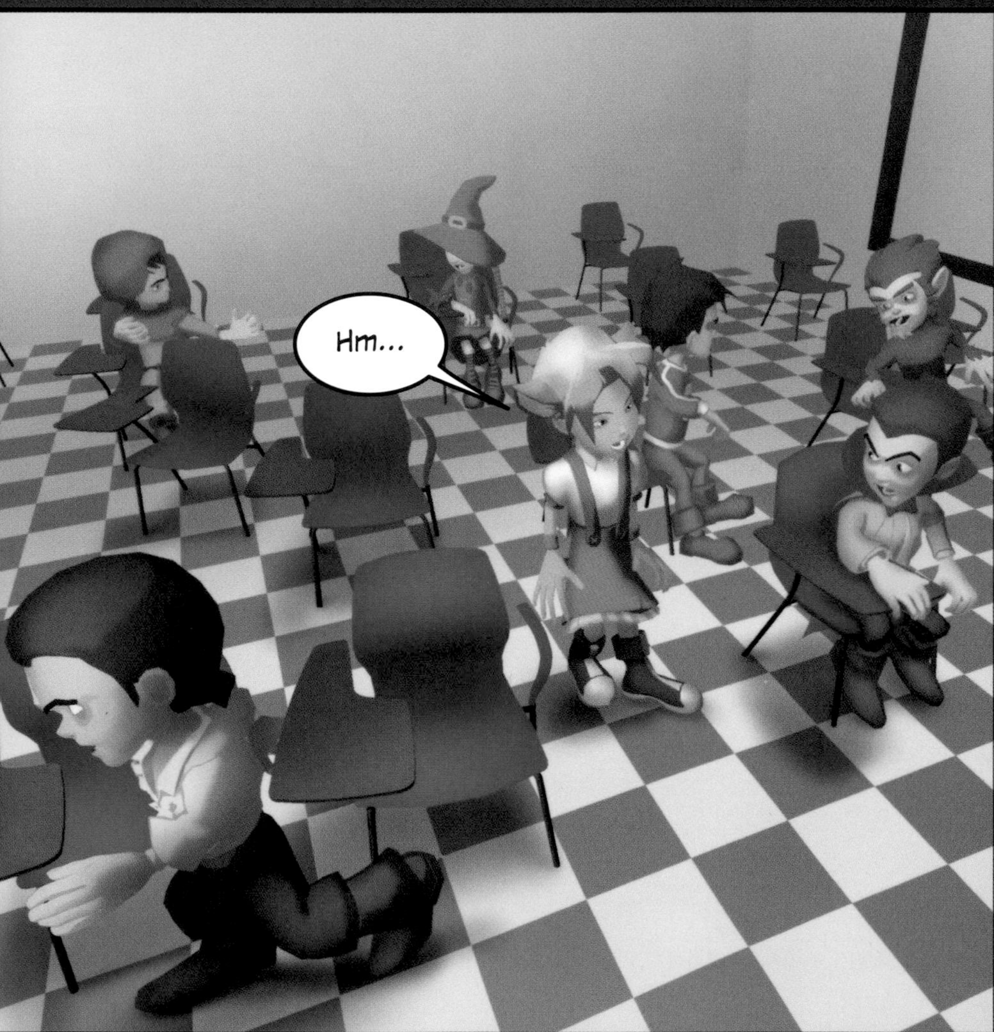
Hm...

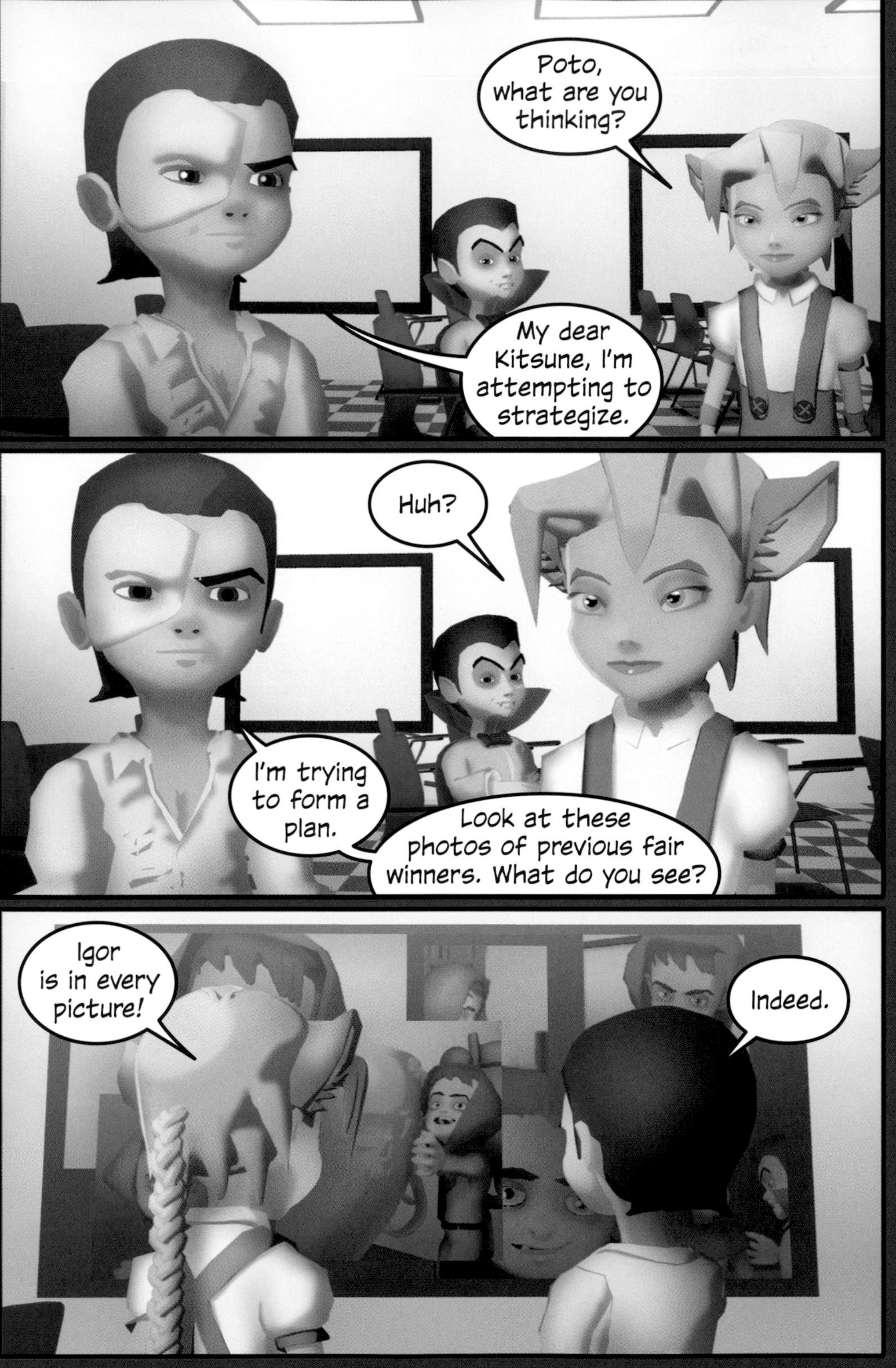
Poto, what are you thinking?
My dear Kitsune, I'm attempting to strategize.
Huh?
I'm trying to form a plan.
Look at these photos of previous fair winners. What do you see?
Igor is in every picture!
Indeed.

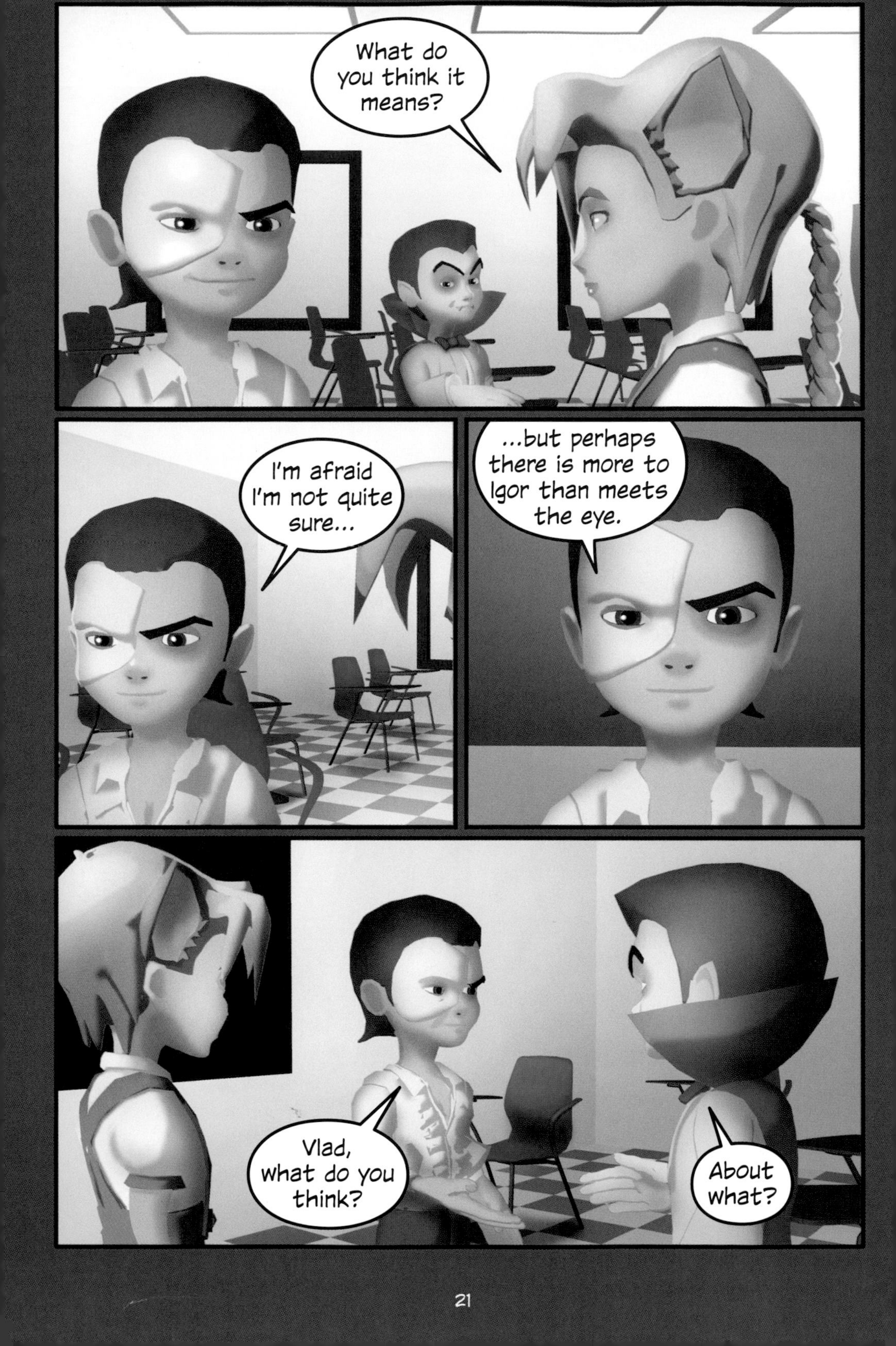
What do you think it means?
I'm afraid I'm not quite sure...
...but perhaps there is more to Igor than meets the eye.
Vlad, what do you think?
About what?

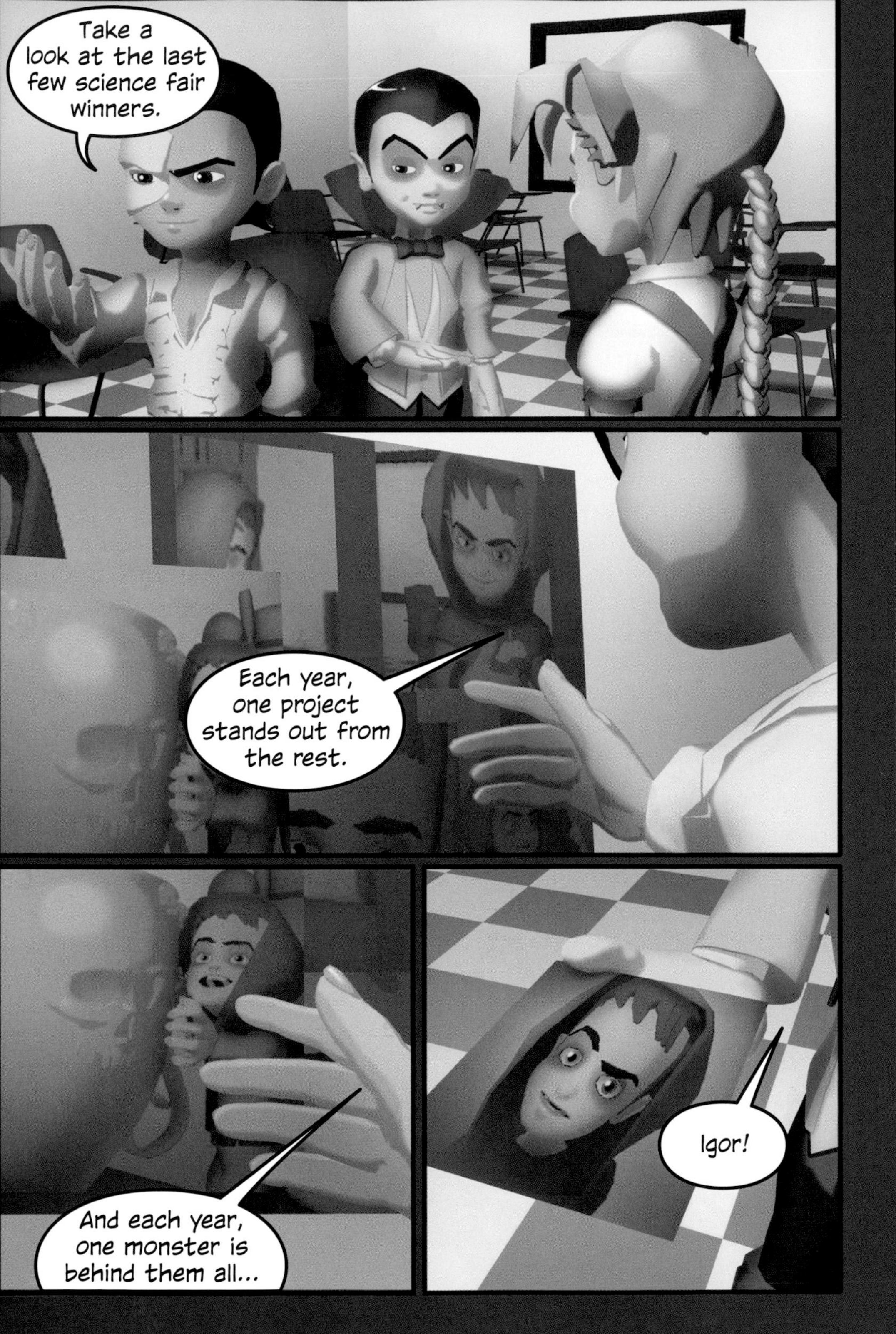
Take a look at the last few science fair winners.
Each year, one project stands out from the rest.
And each year, one monster is behind them all...
Igor!

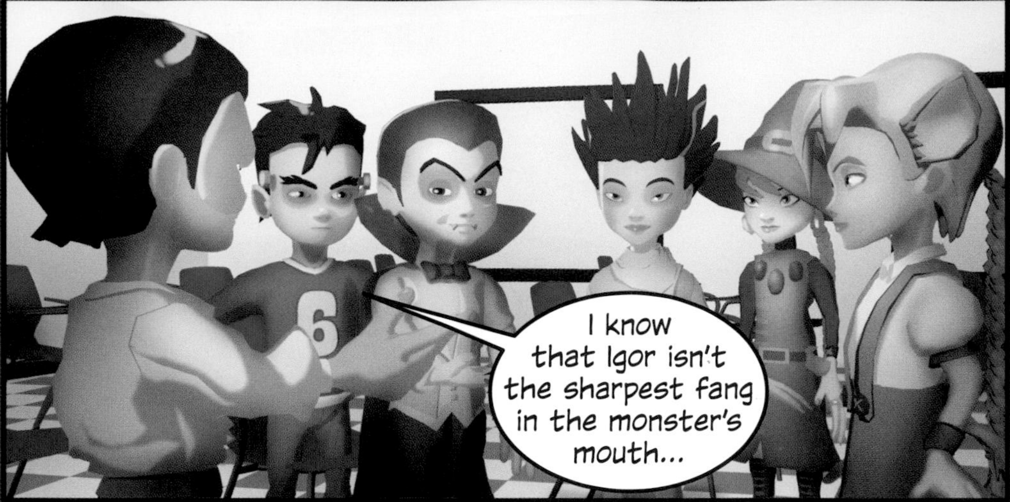
I know that Igor isn't the sharpest fang in the monster's mouth...
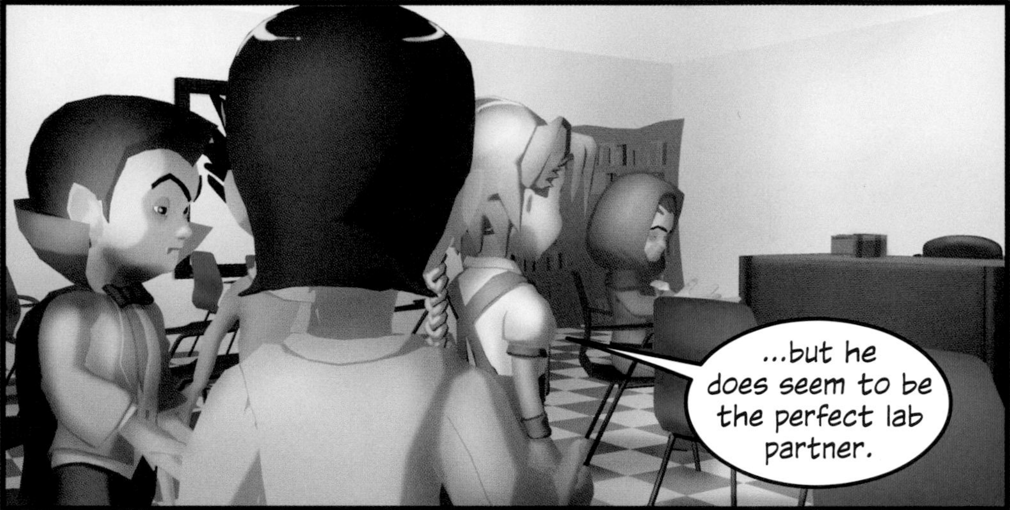
...but he does seem to be the perfect lab partner.
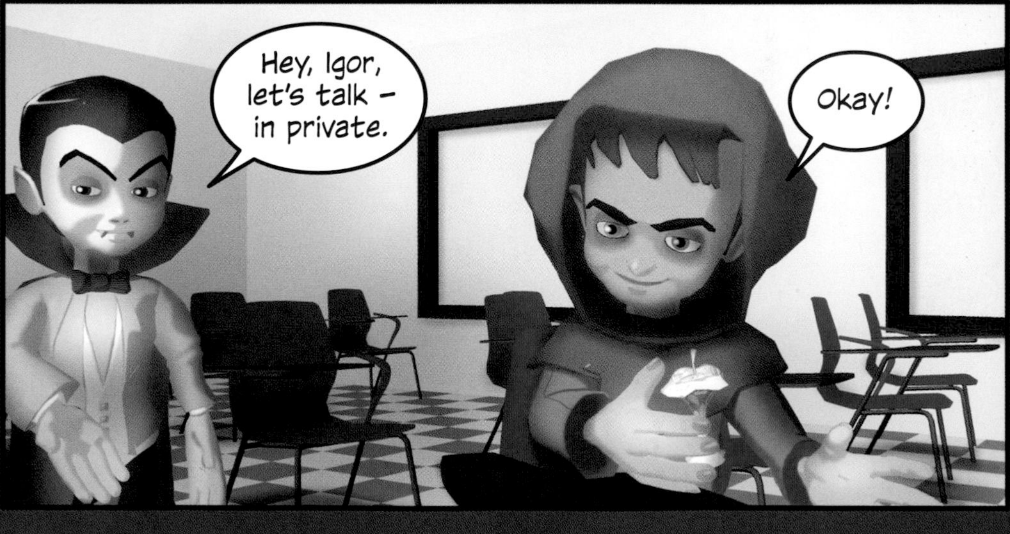
Hey, Igor, let's talk – in private.
Okay!

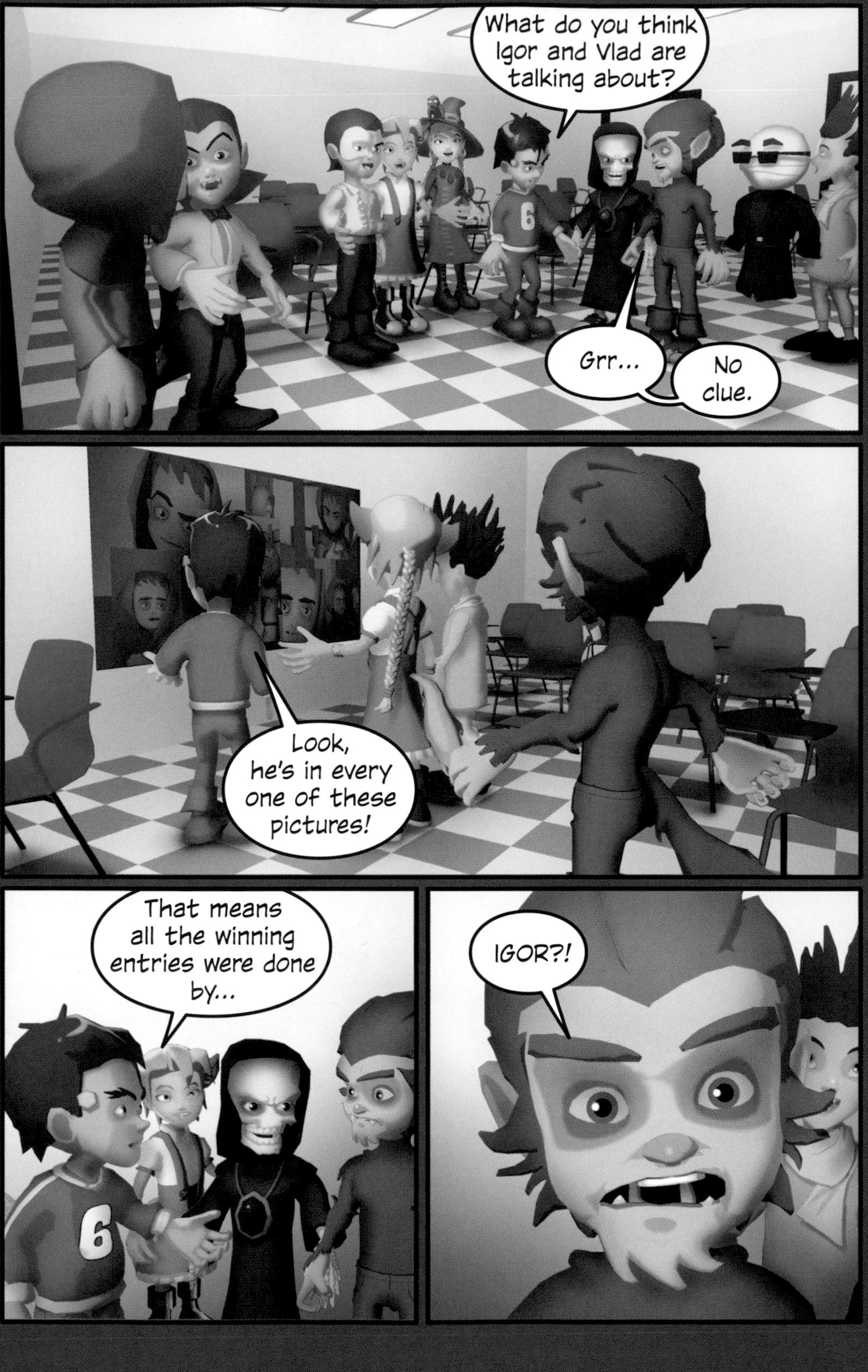
What do you think Igor and Vlad are talking about?
Grr...
No clue.
Look, he's in every one of these pictures!
That means all the winning entries were done by...
IGOR?!

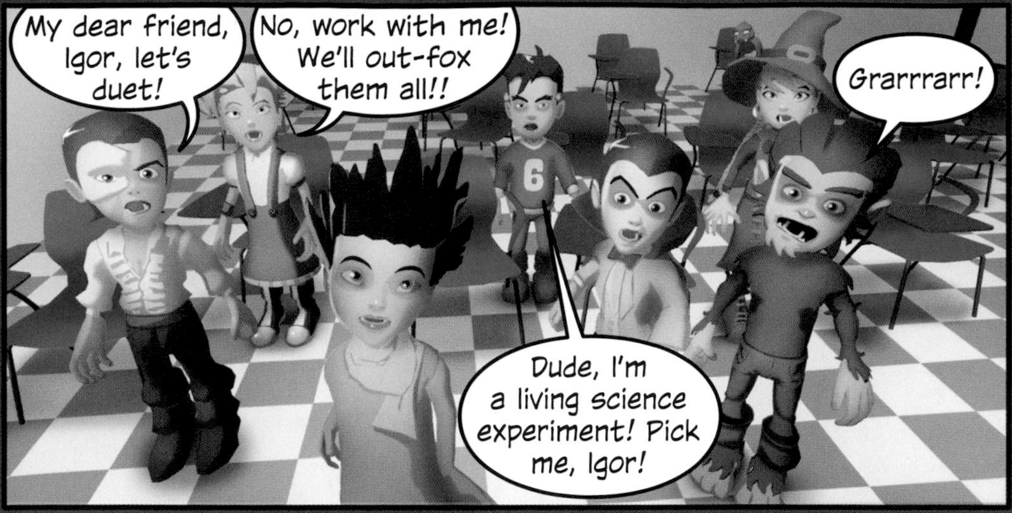
My dear friend, Igor, let's duet!
No, work with me! We'll out-fox them all!!
Grarrrarr!
Dude, I'm a living science experiment! Pick me, Igor!

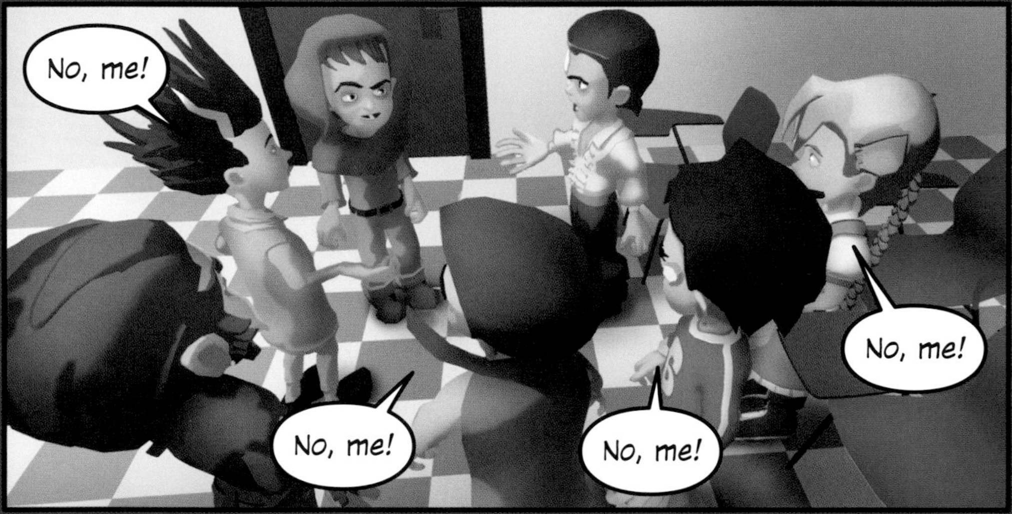
No, me!
No, me!
No, me!
No, me!

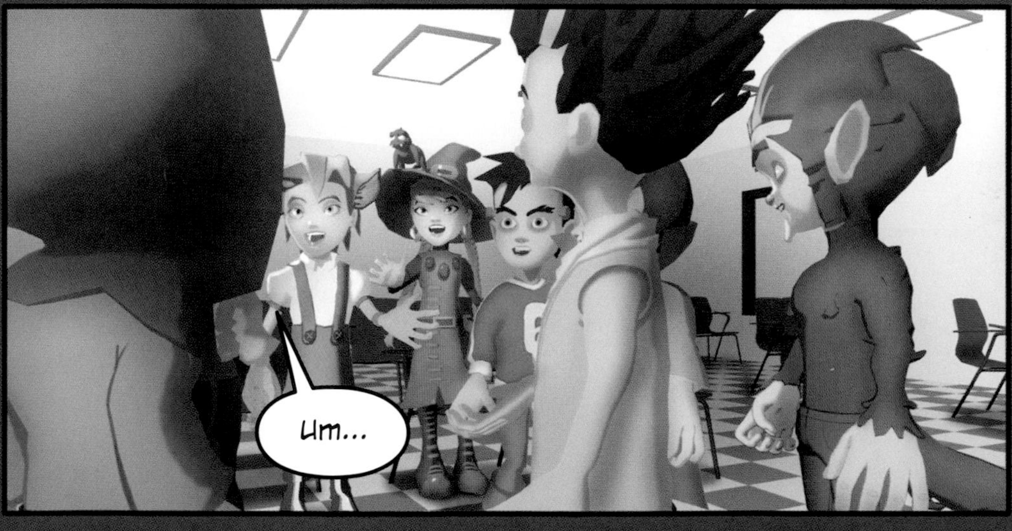
Um...

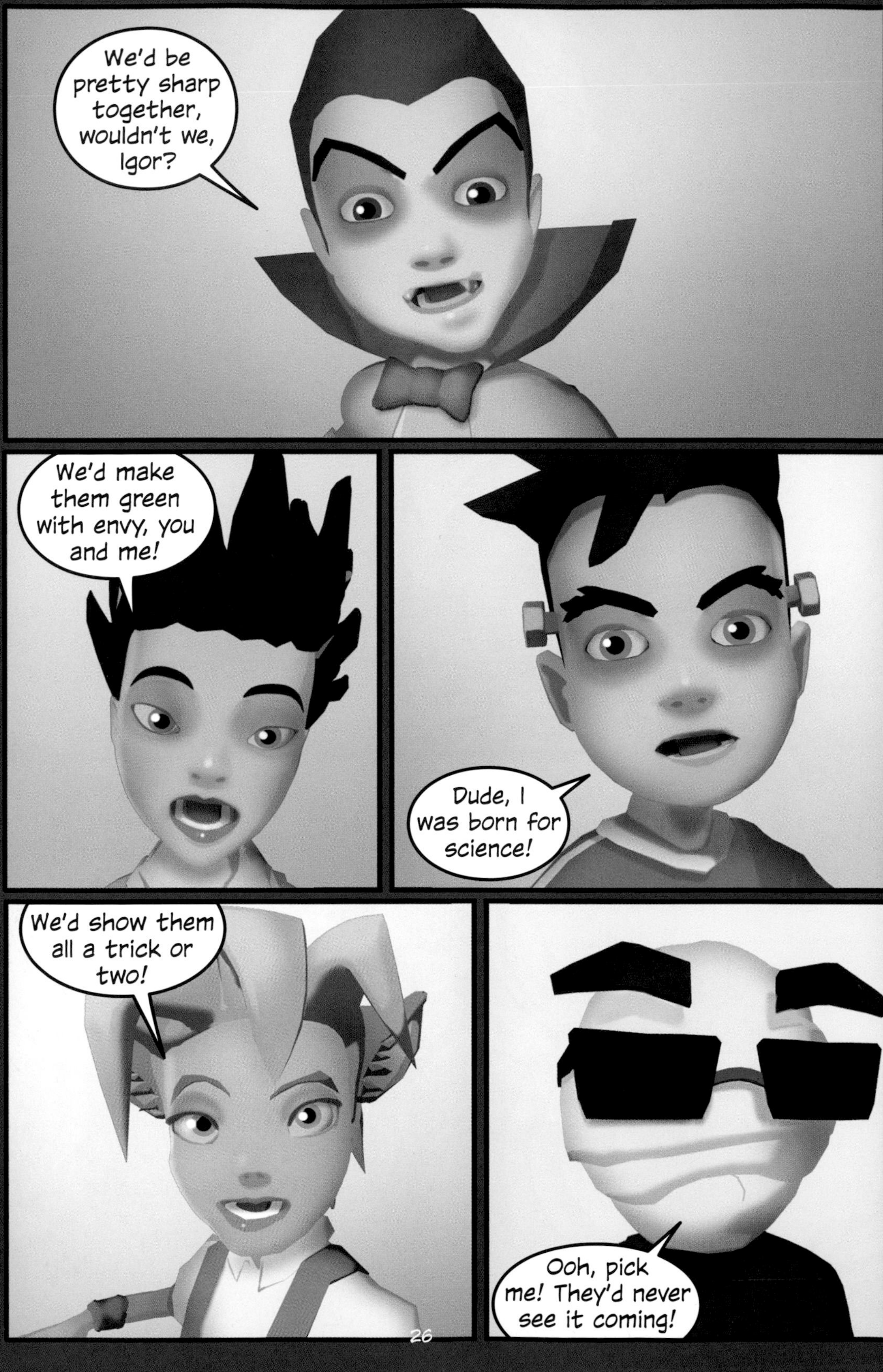
We'd be pretty sharp together, wouldn't we, Igor?
We'd make them green with envy, you and me!
Dude, I was born for science!
We'd show them all a trick or two!
Ooh, pick me! They'd never see it coming!

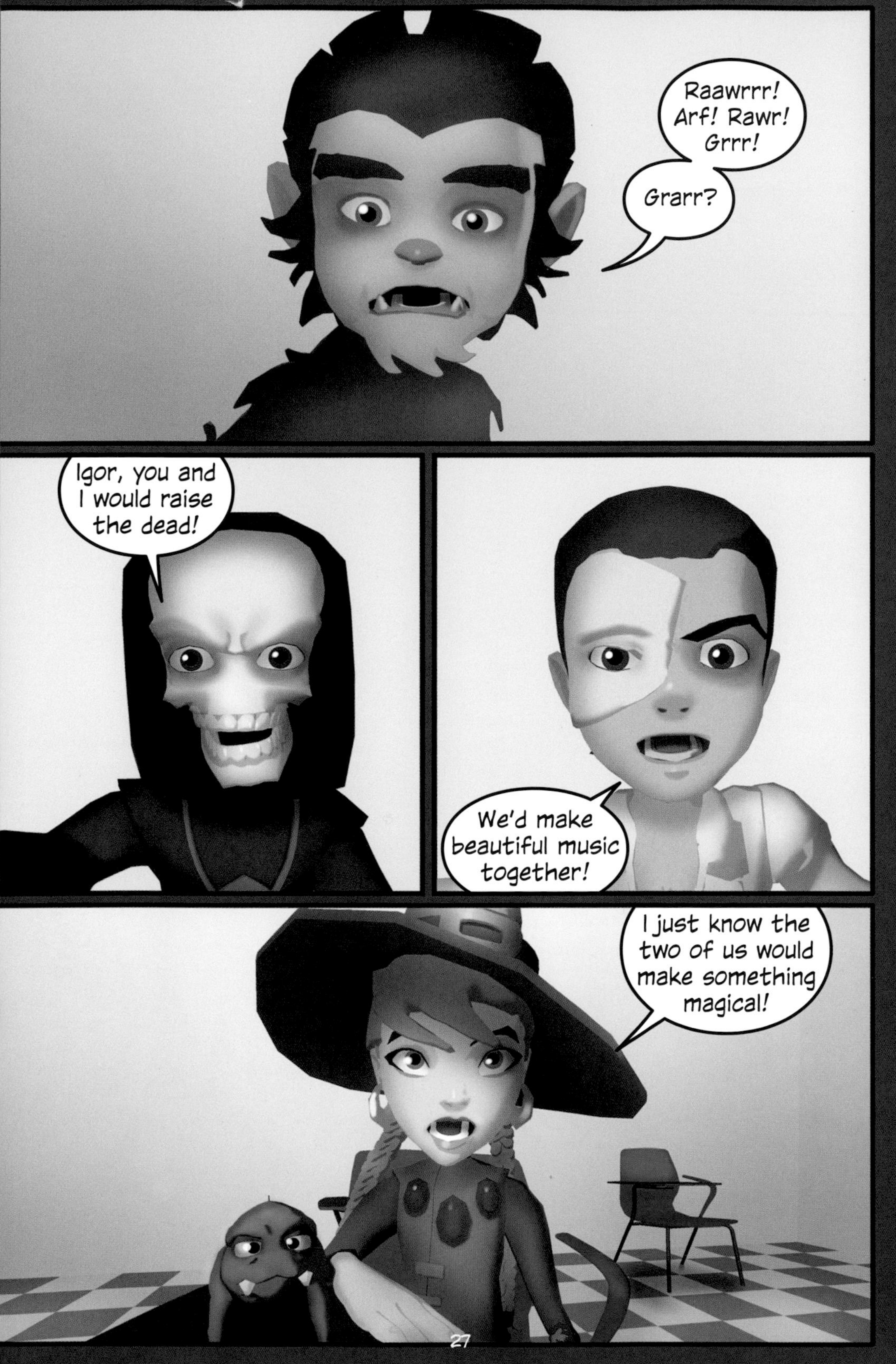
Raawrrr! Arf! Rawr! Grrr!
Grarr?
Igor, you and I would raise the dead!
We'd make beautiful music together!
I just know the two of us would make something magical!

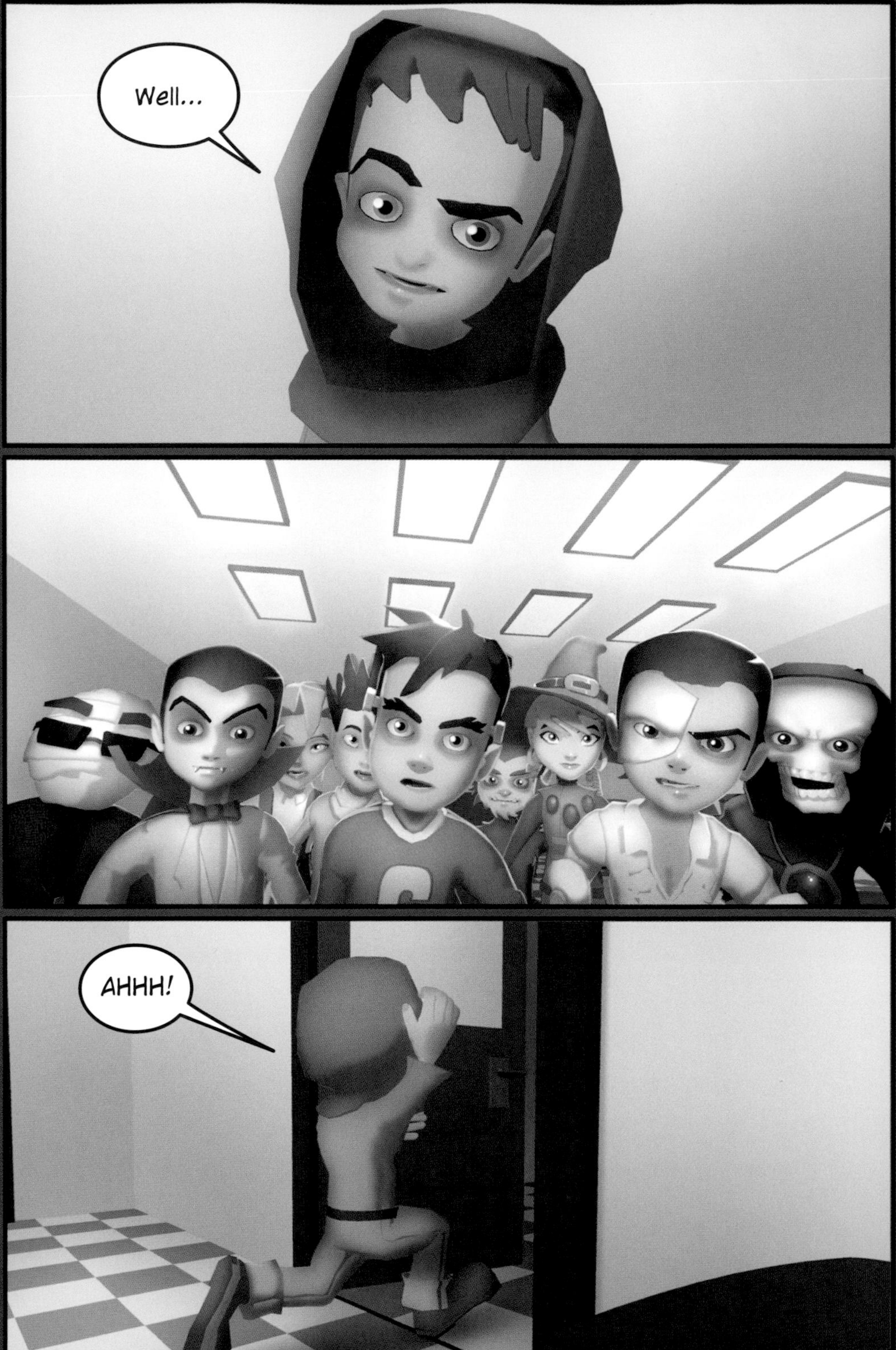
Well...
AHHH!

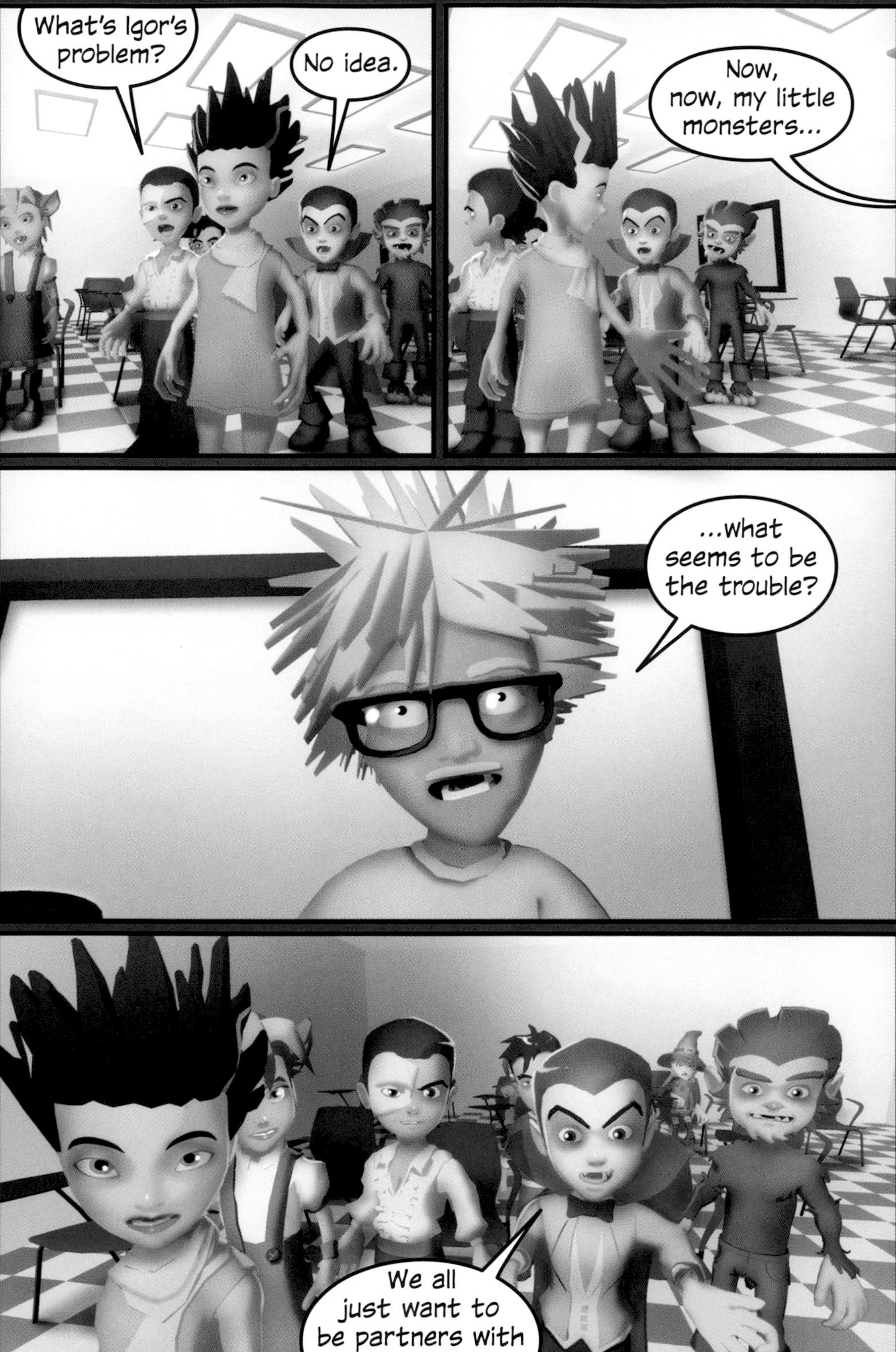
What's Igor's problem?
No idea.
Now, now, my little monsters...
...what seems to be the trouble?
We all just want to be partners with Igor, Mr. West.

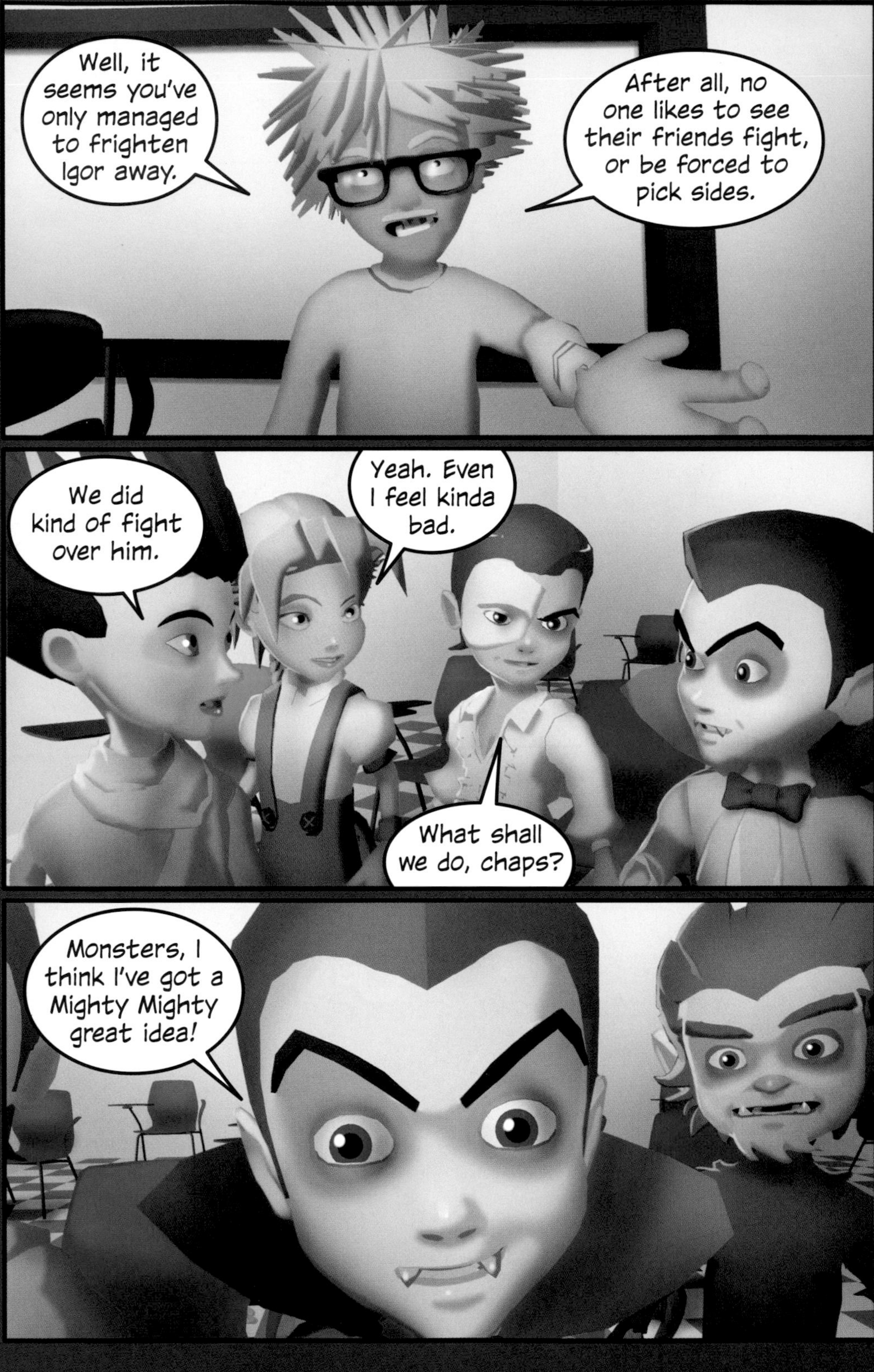
Well, it seems you've only managed to frighten Igor away.
After all, no one likes to see their friends fight, or be forced to pick sides.
We did kind of fight over him.
Yeah. Even I feel kinda bad.
What shall we do, chaps?
Monsters, I think I've got a Mighty Mighty great idea!

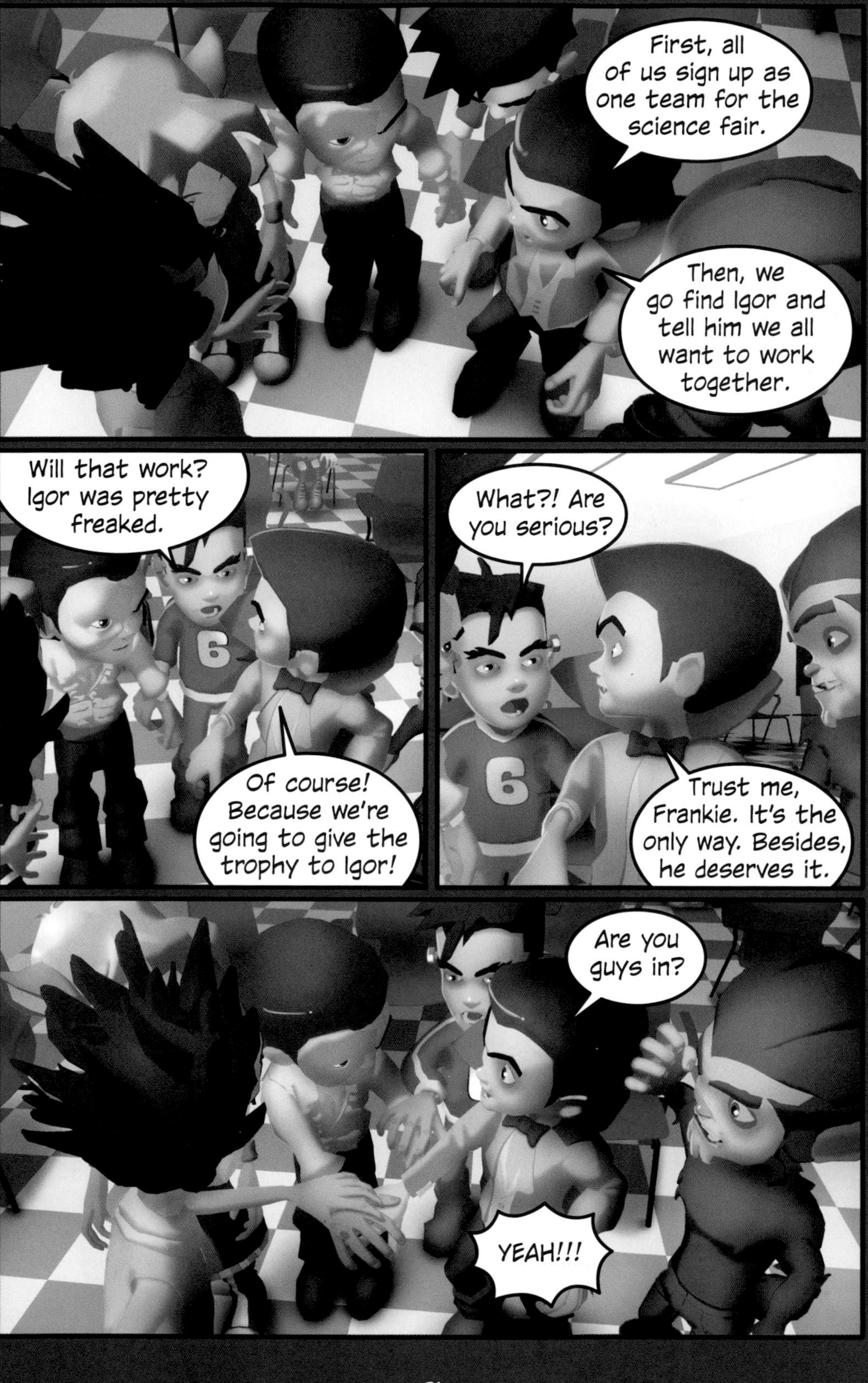
First, all of us sign up as one team for the science fair.
Then, we go find Igor and tell him we all want to work together.
Will that work? Igor was pretty freaked.
Of course! Because we're going to give the trophy to Igor!
What?! Are you serious?
Trust me, Frankie. It's the only way. Besides, he deserves it.
Are you guys in?
YEAH!!!

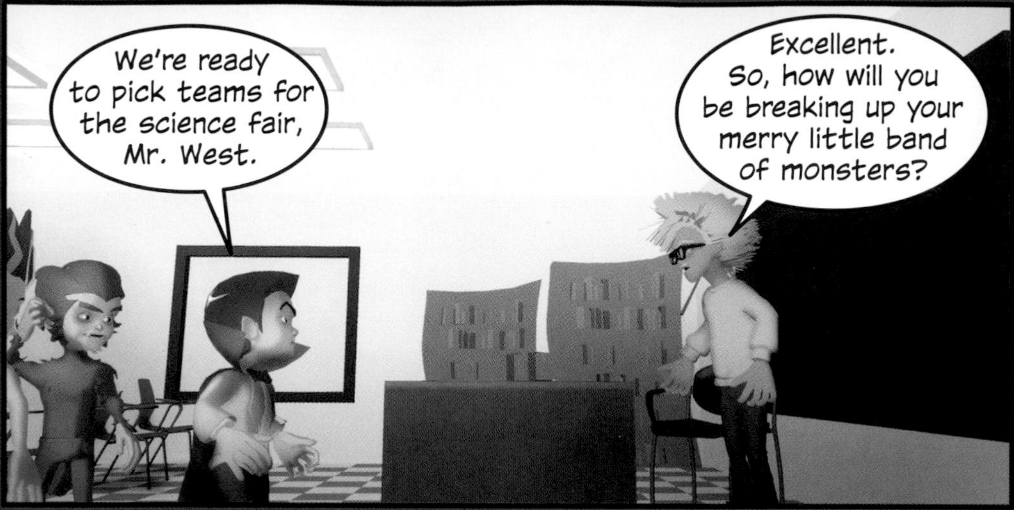
We're ready to pick teams for the science fair, Mr. West.
Excellent. So, how will you be breaking up your merry little band of monsters?

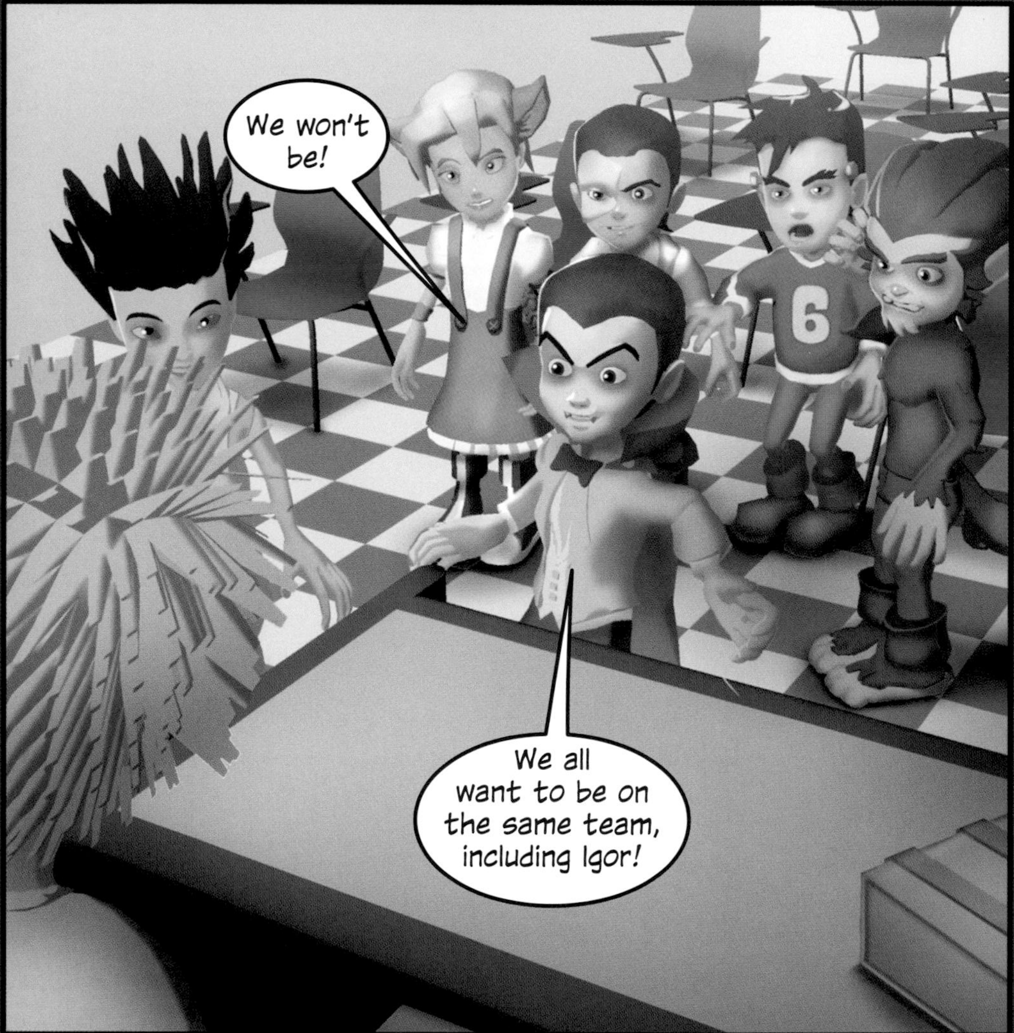
We won't be!
We all want to be on the same team, including Igor!

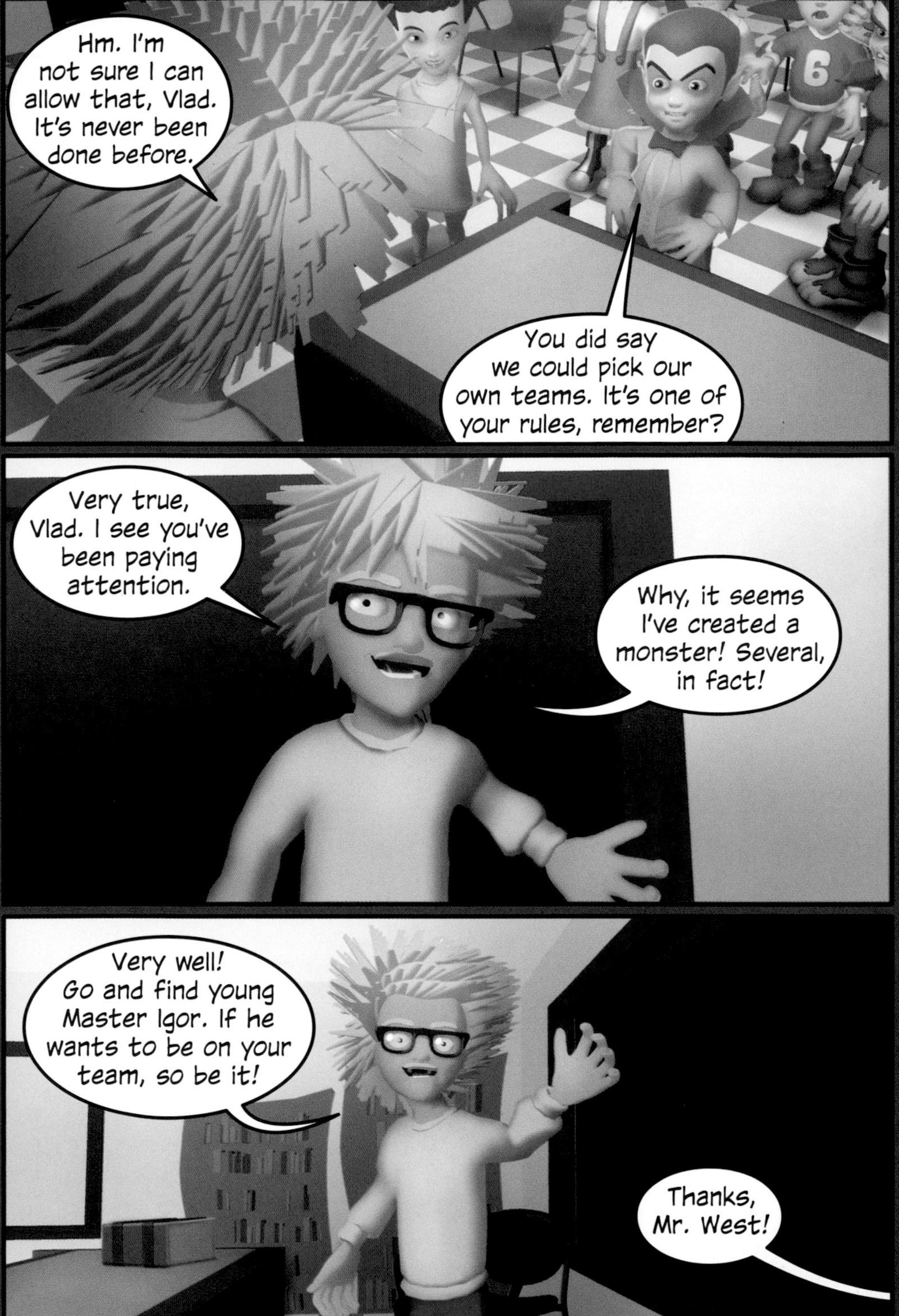
Hm. I'm not sure I can allow that, Vlad. It's never been done before.
You did say we could pick our own teams. It's one of your rules, remember?
Very true, Vlad. I see you've been paying attention.
Why, it seems I've created a monster! Several, in fact!
Very well! Go and find young Master Igor. If he wants to be on your team, so be it!
Thanks, Mr. West!

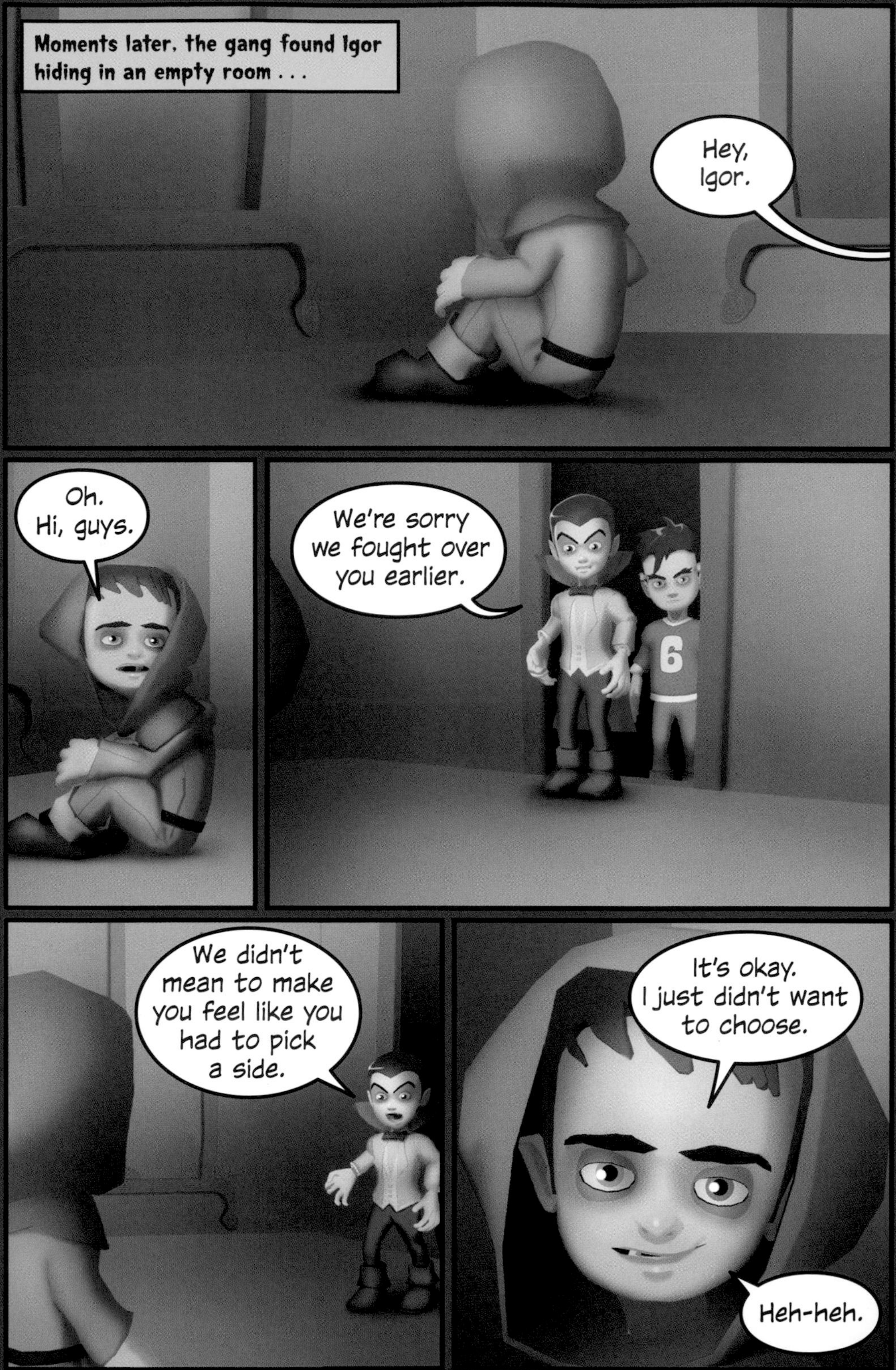
Moments later, the gang found Igor hiding in an empty room . . .
Hey, Igor.
Oh. Hi, guys.
We're sorry we fought over you earlier.
We didn't mean to make you feel like you had to pick a side.
It's okay. I just didn't want to choose.
Heh-heh.

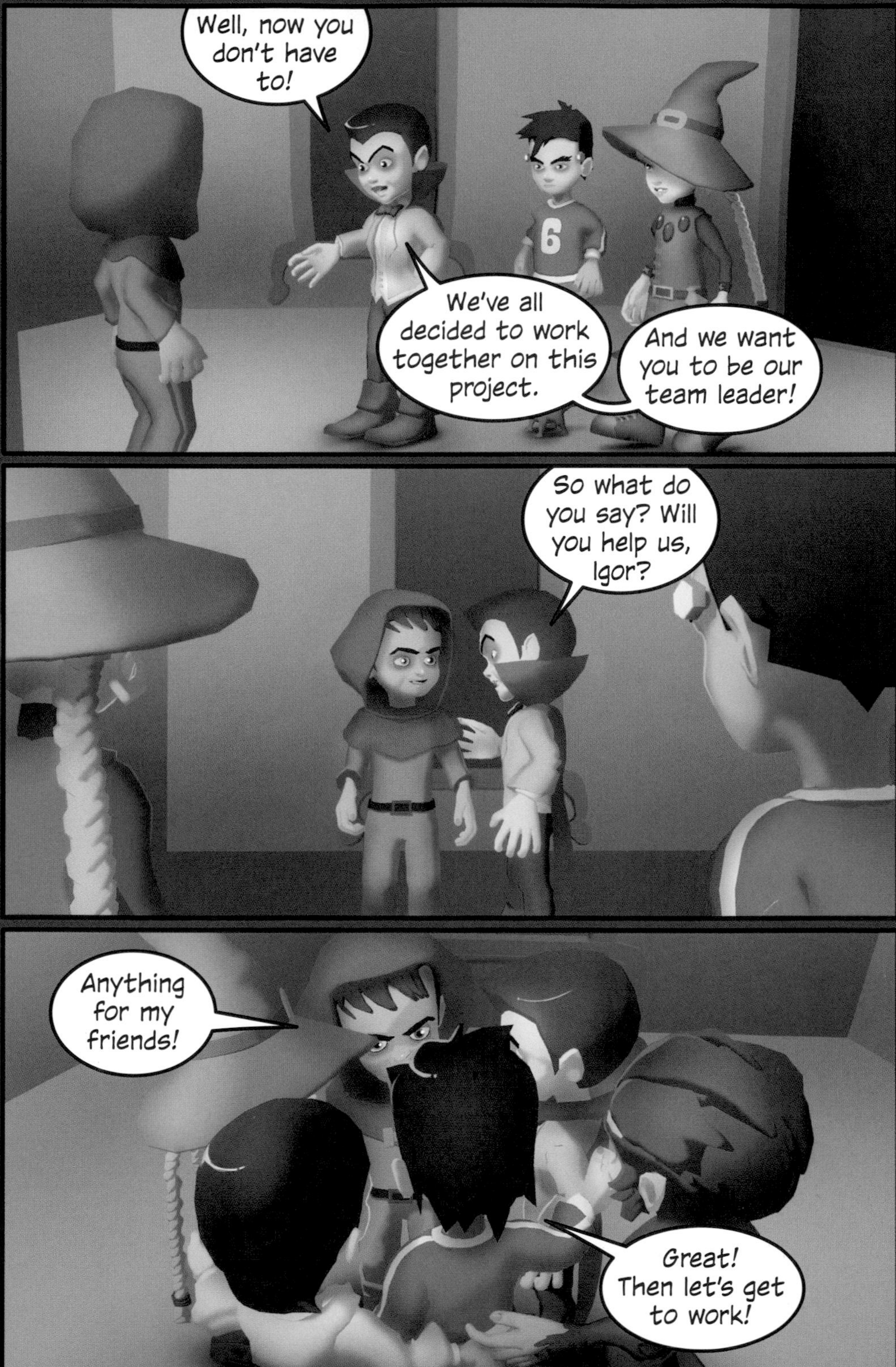
Well, now you don't have to!
We've all decided to work together on this project.
And we want you to be our team leader!
So what do you say? Will you help us, Igor?
Anything for my friends!
Great! Then let's get to work!

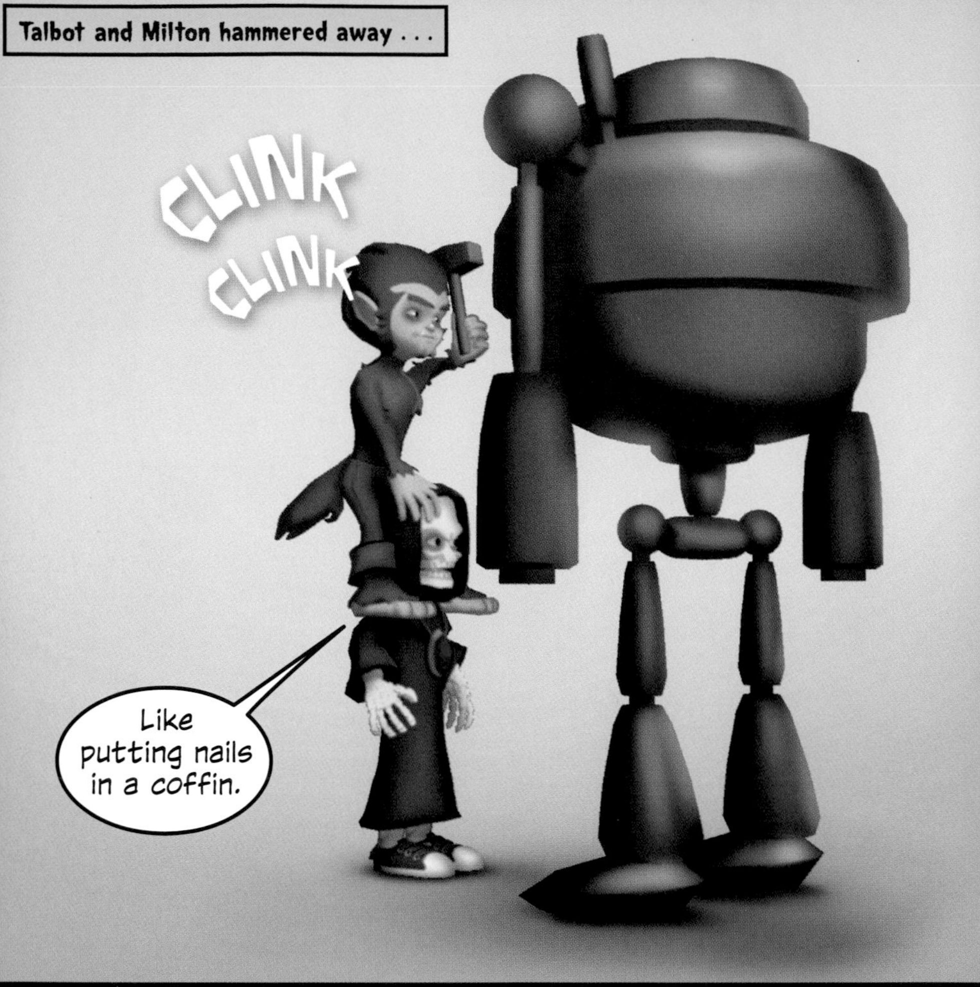
Talbot and Milton hammered away . . .
CLINK
CLINK
Like putting nails in a coffin.

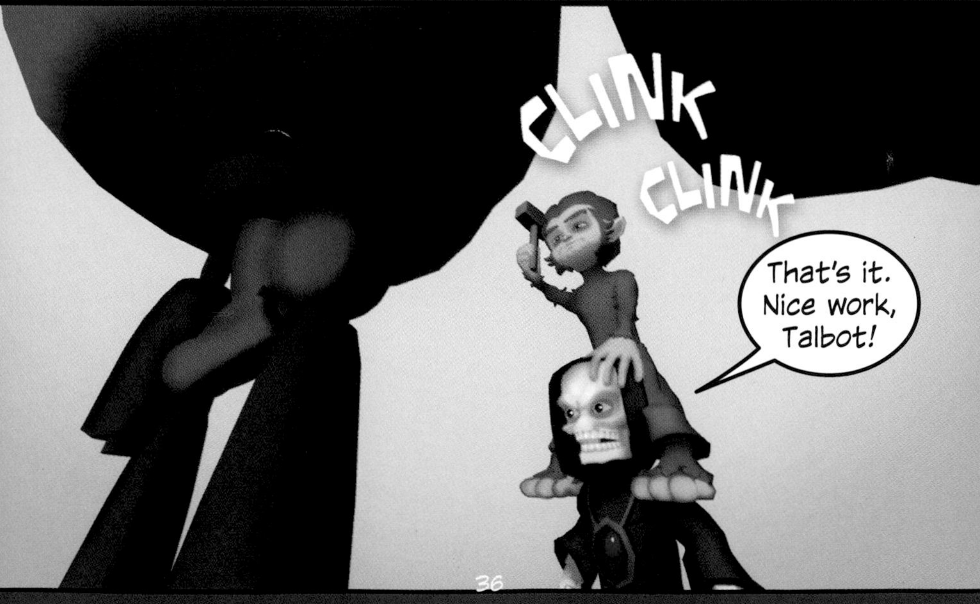
CLINK
CLINK
That's it. Nice work, Talbot!

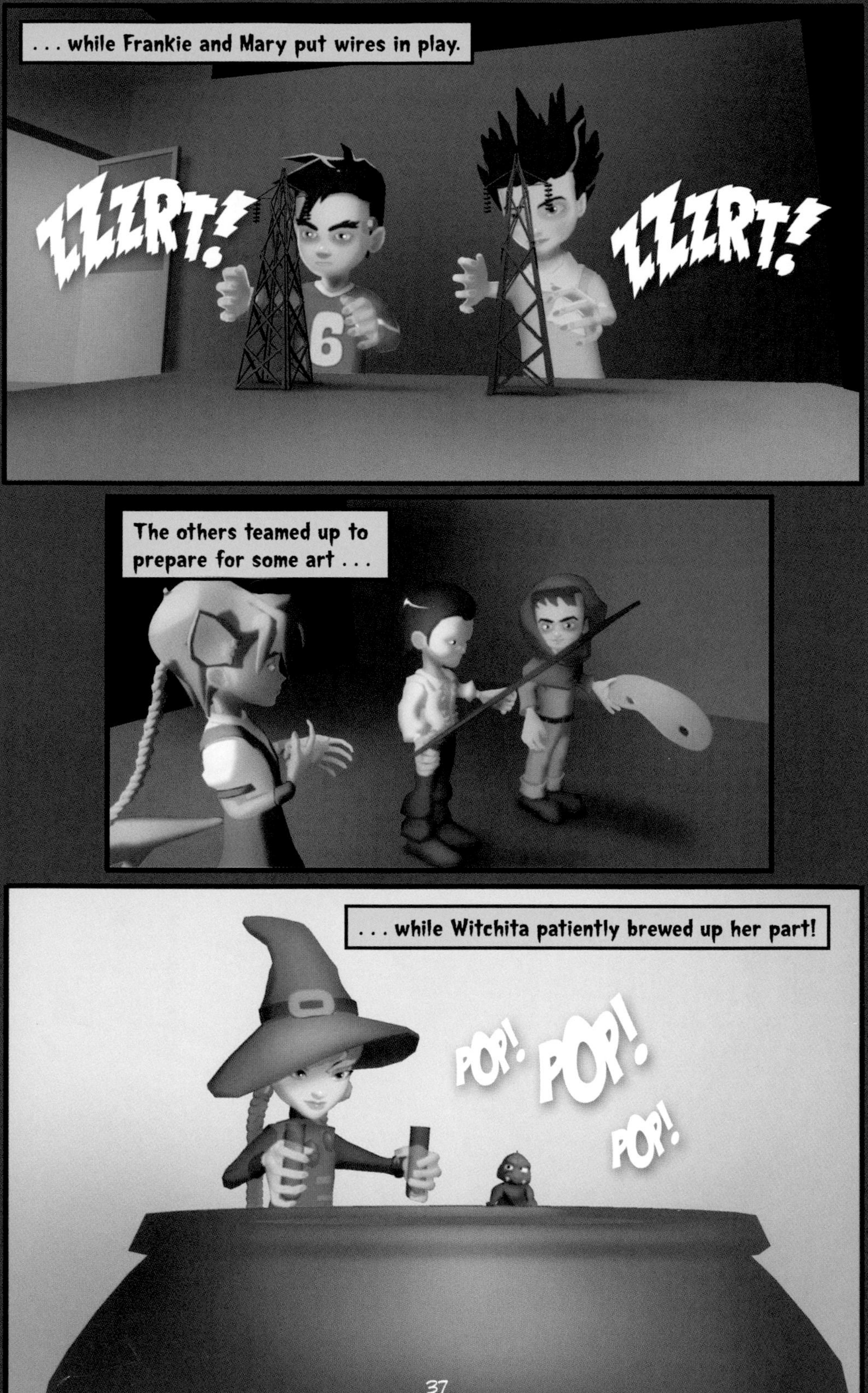

. . . while Frankie and Mary put wires in play.
ZZZRT!
ZZZRT!
The others teamed up to prepare for some art . . .
. . . while Witchita patiently brewed up her part!
POP!
POP!
POP!

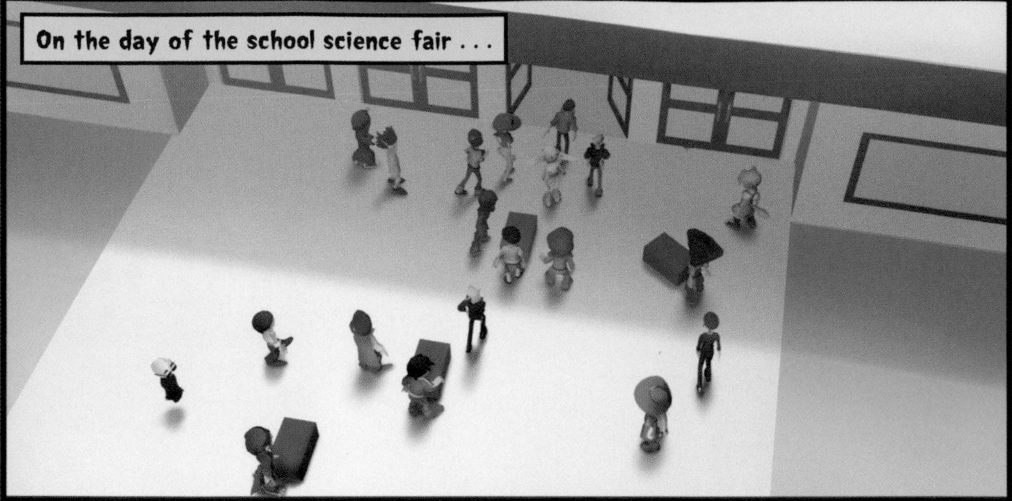
On the day of the school science fair . . .

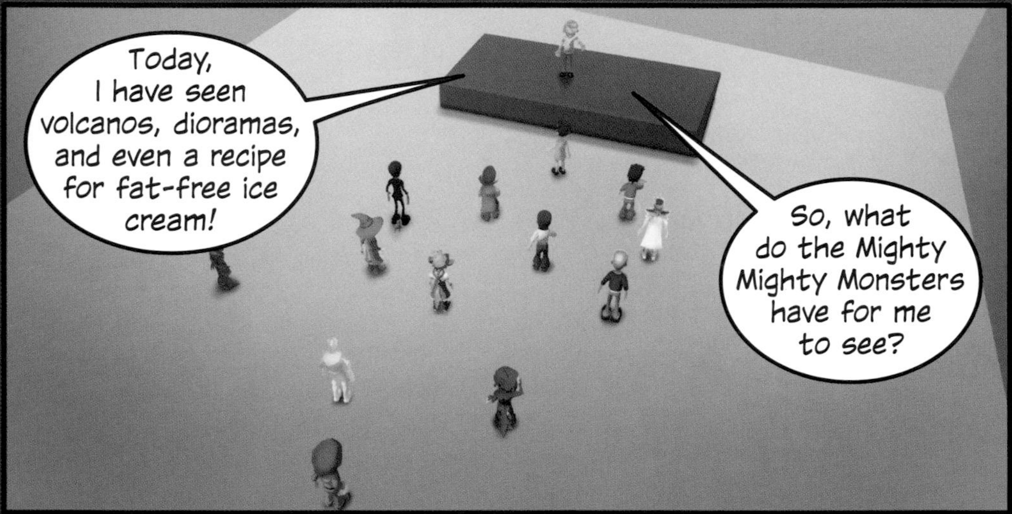
Today, I have seen volcanos, dioramas, and even a recipe for fat-free ice cream!
So, what do the Mighty Mighty Monsters have for me to see?

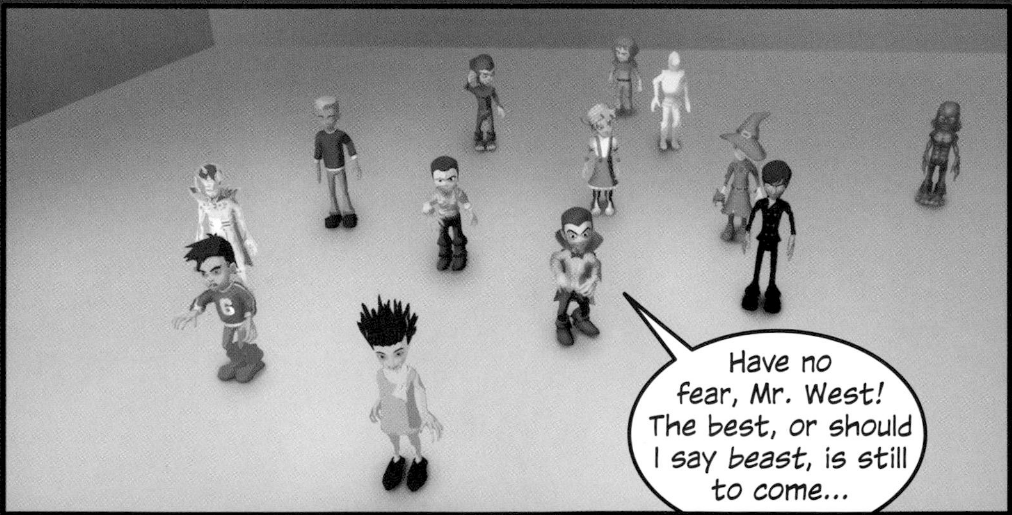
Have no fear, Mr. West! The best, or should I say *beast*, is still to come...

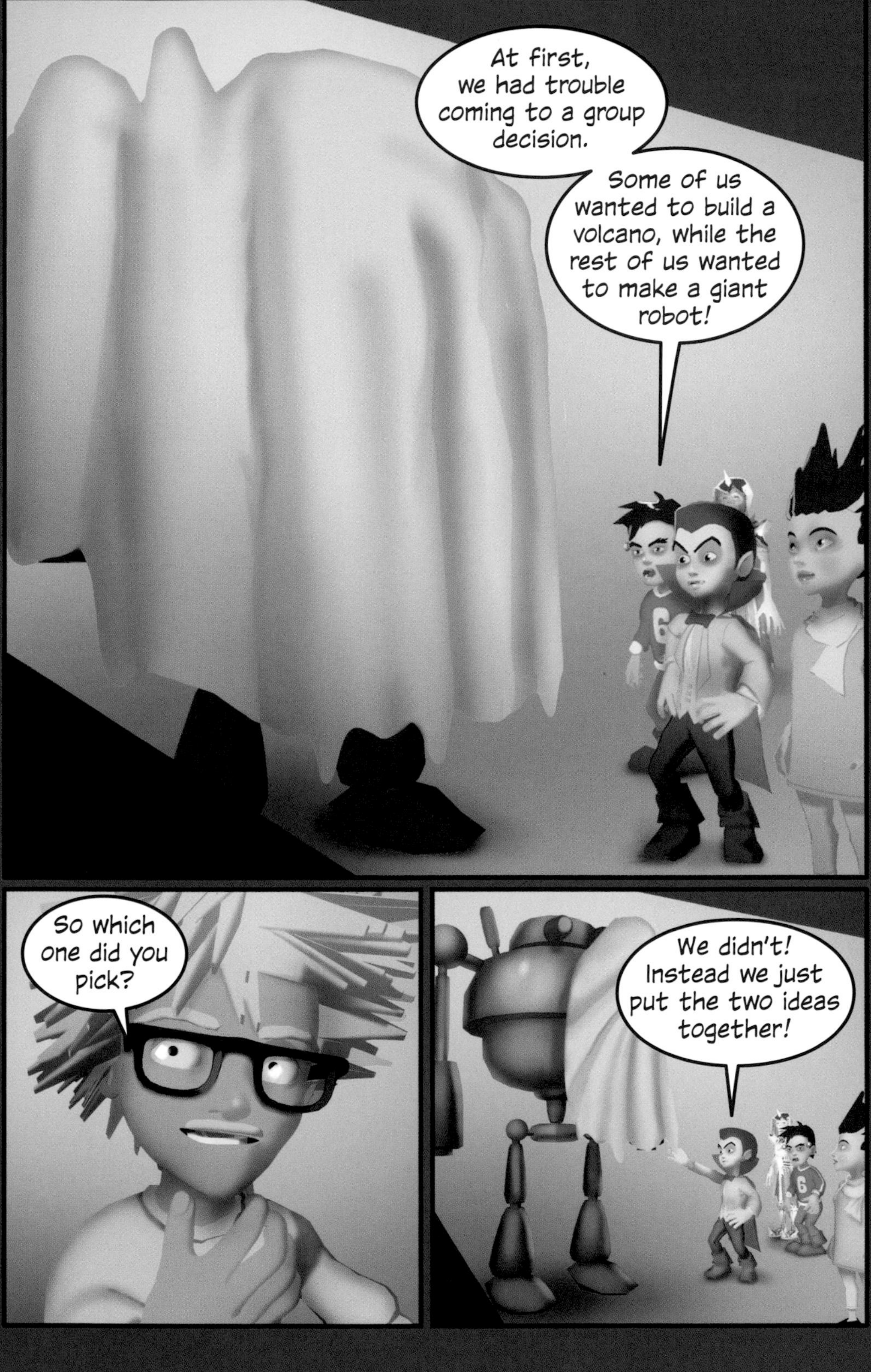
At first, we had trouble coming to a group decision.
Some of us wanted to build a volcano, while the rest of us wanted to make a giant robot!
So which one did you pick?
We didn't! Instead we just put the two ideas together!

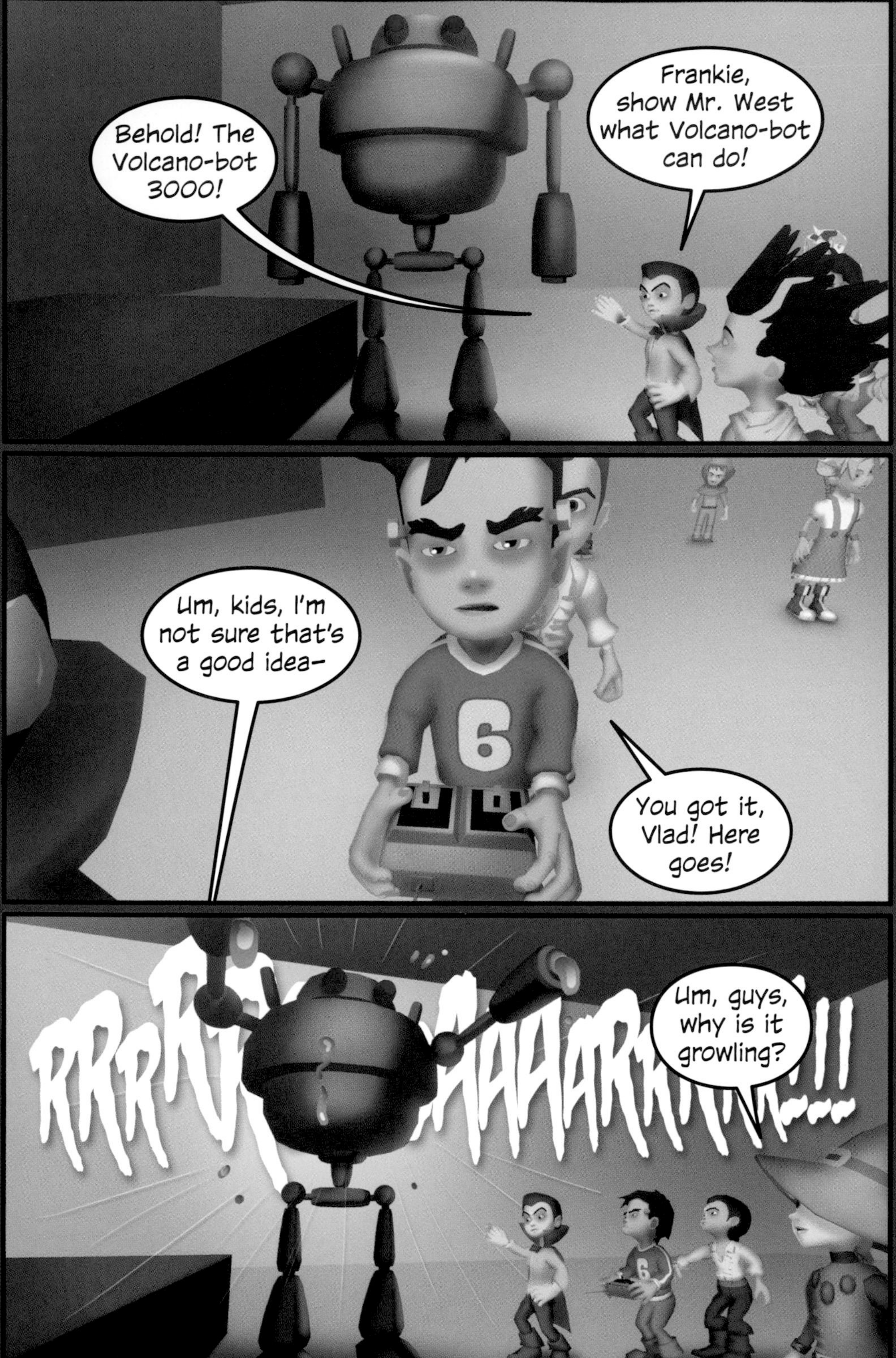
Behold! The Volcano-bot 3000!
Frankie, show Mr. West what Volcano-bot can do!
Um, kids, I'm not sure that's a good idea-
You got it, Vlad! Here goes!
Um, guys, why is it growling?

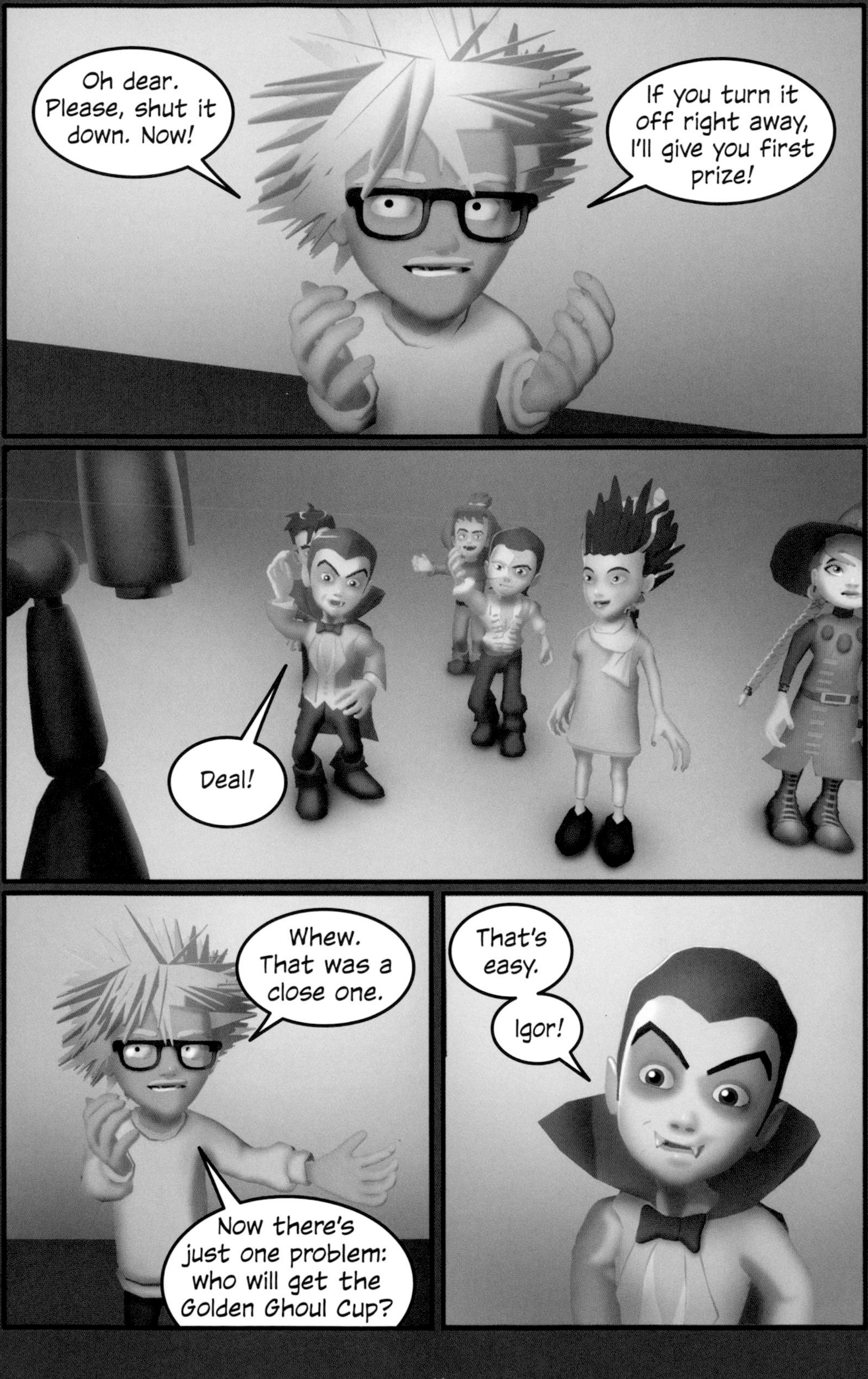
Oh dear. Please, shut it down. Now!
If you turn it off right away, I'll give you first prize!
Deal!
Whew. That was a close one.
Now there's just one problem: who will get the Golden Ghoul Cup?
That's easy.
Igor!

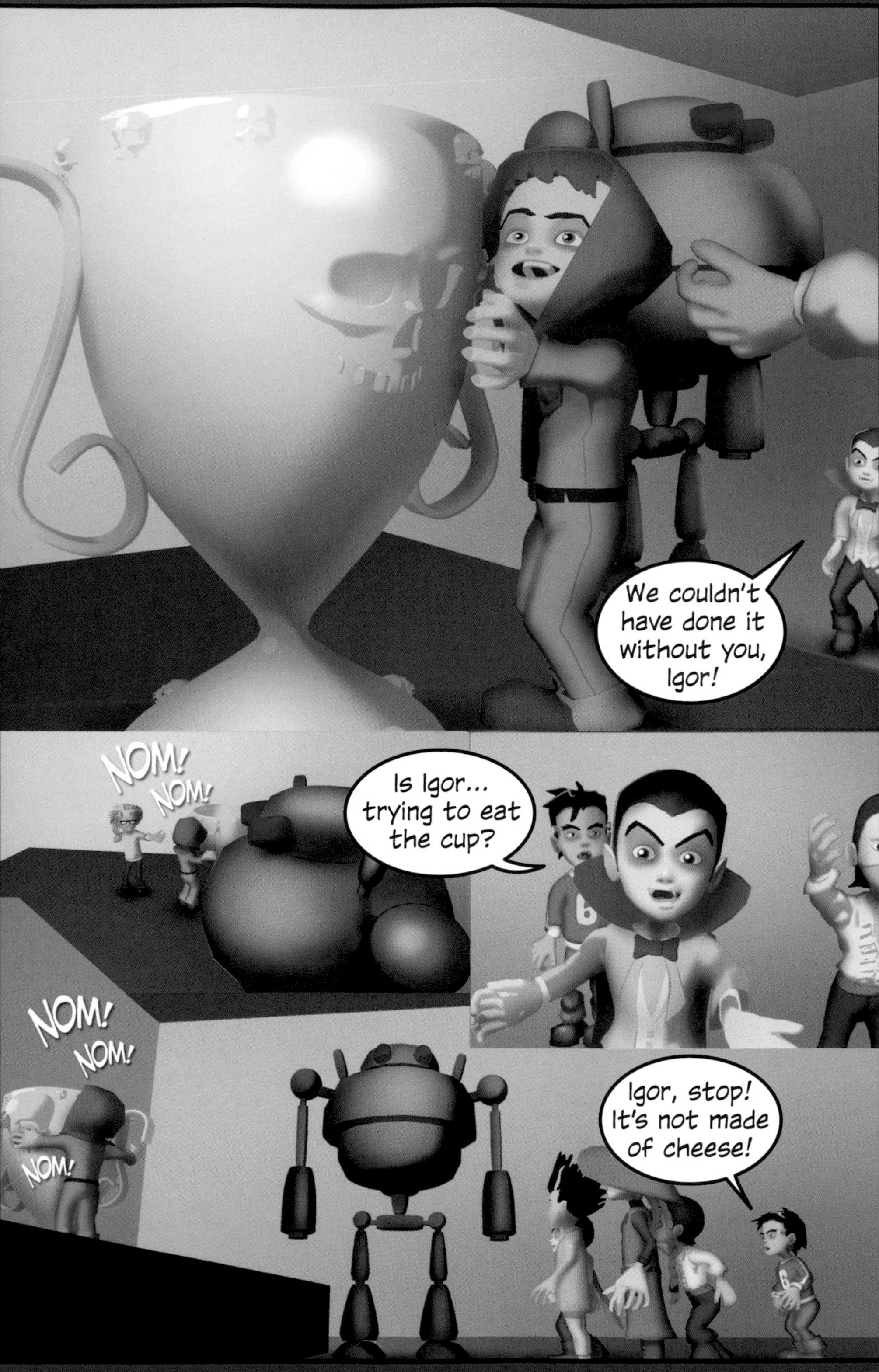
We couldn't have done it without you, Igor!
NOM! NOM!
Is Igor... trying to eat the cup?
NOM! NOM!
NOM!
Igor, stop! It's not made of cheese!

As a lifelong comics fan, Sean O'Reilly dreamed of becoming a comic book creator. In 2004, he realized that dream by creating Arcana Studio. In one short year, O'Reilly took his studio from a one-person operation in his basement to an award-winning comic book publisher with more than 150 graphic novels produced for Harper Collins, Simon & Schuster, Random House, Scholastic, and others.

Within a year, the company won many awards including the Shuster Award for Outstanding Publisher and the Moonbeam Award for top children's graphic novel. O'Reilly also won the Top 40 Under 40 award from the city of Vancouver and authored The Clockwork Girl for Top Graphic Novel at Book Expo America in 2009. Currently, O'Reilly is one of the most prolific independent comic book writers in Canada. While showing no signs of slowing down in comics, he now writes screenplays and adapts his creations for the big screen.

GLOSSARY

dioramas (dye-uh-RAH-muhz)—life-sized displays featuring things from nature, or science projects

disaster (duh-ZASS-tur)—an event that causes great damage, loss, or suffering

duet (doo-ET)—a piece of music or a song that is performed by two singers

envy (EN-vee)—when you envy someone, you want what that person has

experiment (ek-SPER-uh-ment)—a scientific test to try out a theory or to see the effect of something

forced (FORSSD)—made someone do something

ghoul (GOOL)—an evil creature that feeds on human beings

potions (POH-shuhnz)—a drinkable medicinal or magical liquid

previous (PREE-vee-uhss)—former, or happening before

strategize (STRAT-uh-jize)—if you strategize, you try to create a clever plan to get something done

DISCUSSION QUESTIONS

1. Why did Igor run away screaming from his friends? What do you think bothered him about the situation? Talk about it.

2. The reward for winning the Science Fair is the Golden Ghoul Cup. What kind of prize would you want for winning a contest? Why?

3. Igor's a great lab assistant. What are you good at? Talk about your talents.

WRITING PROMPTS

1. Mr. West is the Mighty Mighty Monsters' favorite teacher. Who is your favorite teacher? Why? Write about your favorite teacher.

2. Think up your own science fair experiment. What would your experiment do? What would it prove? Write about your science experiment.

3. If you were one of the Mighty Mighty Monsters, what type of monster would you be? Write a paragraph about your new identity as a monster, then draw a picture of your monstrous self.

Mighty Mighty MONSTERS ADVENTURES

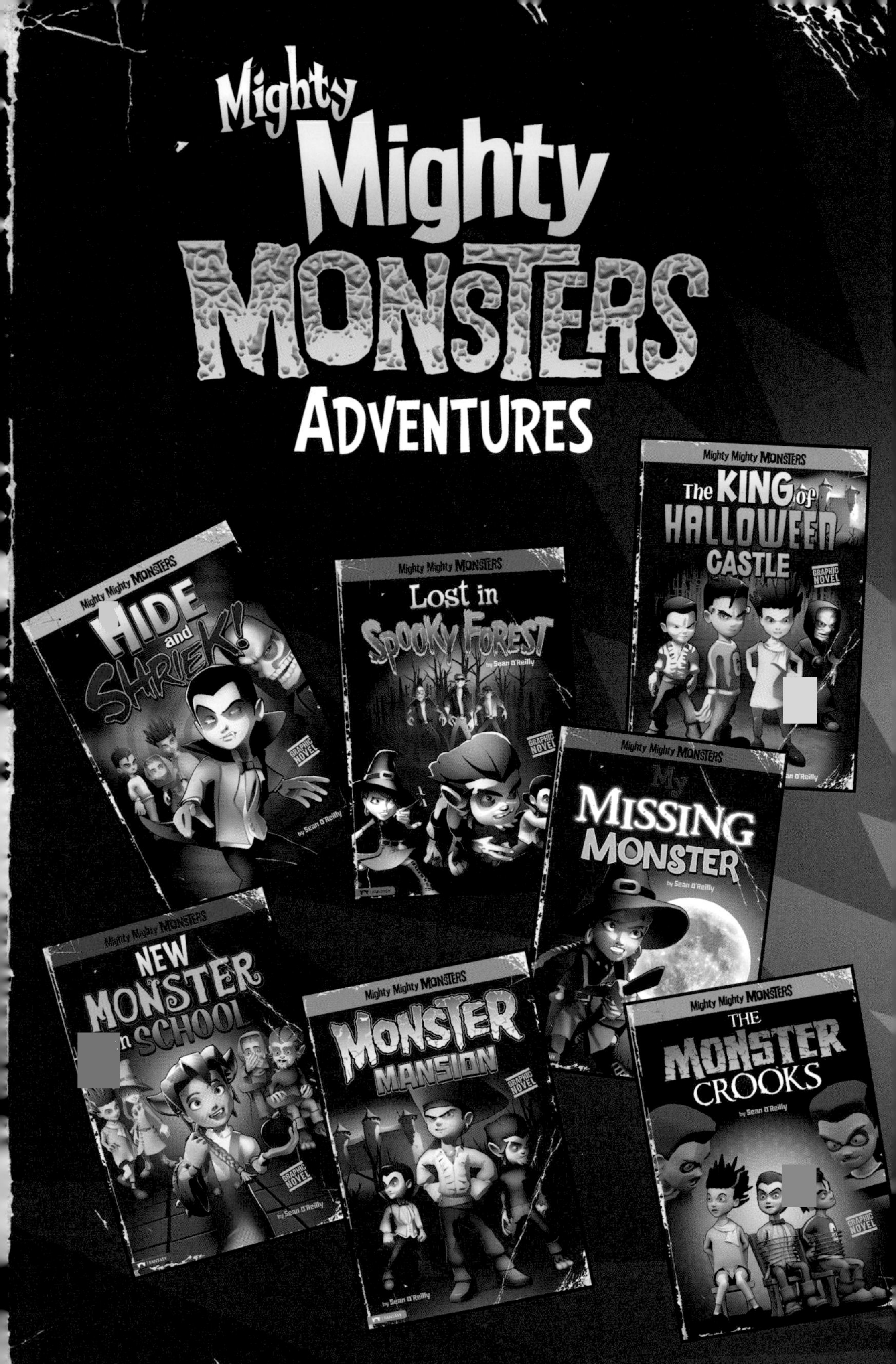
Mighty Mighty MONSTERS
HIDE and SHRIEK!
GRAPHIC NOVEL
by Sean O'Reilly
Mighty Mighty MONSTERS
Lost in Spooky Forest
by Sean O'Reilly
GRAPHIC NOVEL
Mighty Mighty MONSTERS
The KING of HALLOWEEN CASTLE
GRAPHIC NOVEL
Mighty Mighty MONSTERS
My MISSING MONSTER
by Sean O'Reilly
Mighty Mighty MONSTERS
NEW MONSTER in SCHOOL
GRAPHIC NOVEL
by Sean O'Reilly
Mighty Mighty MONSTERS
MONSTER MANSION
GRAPHIC NOVEL
by Sean O'Reilly
Mighty Mighty MONSTERS
THE MONSTER CROOKS
by Sean O'Reilly
GRAPHIC NOVEL

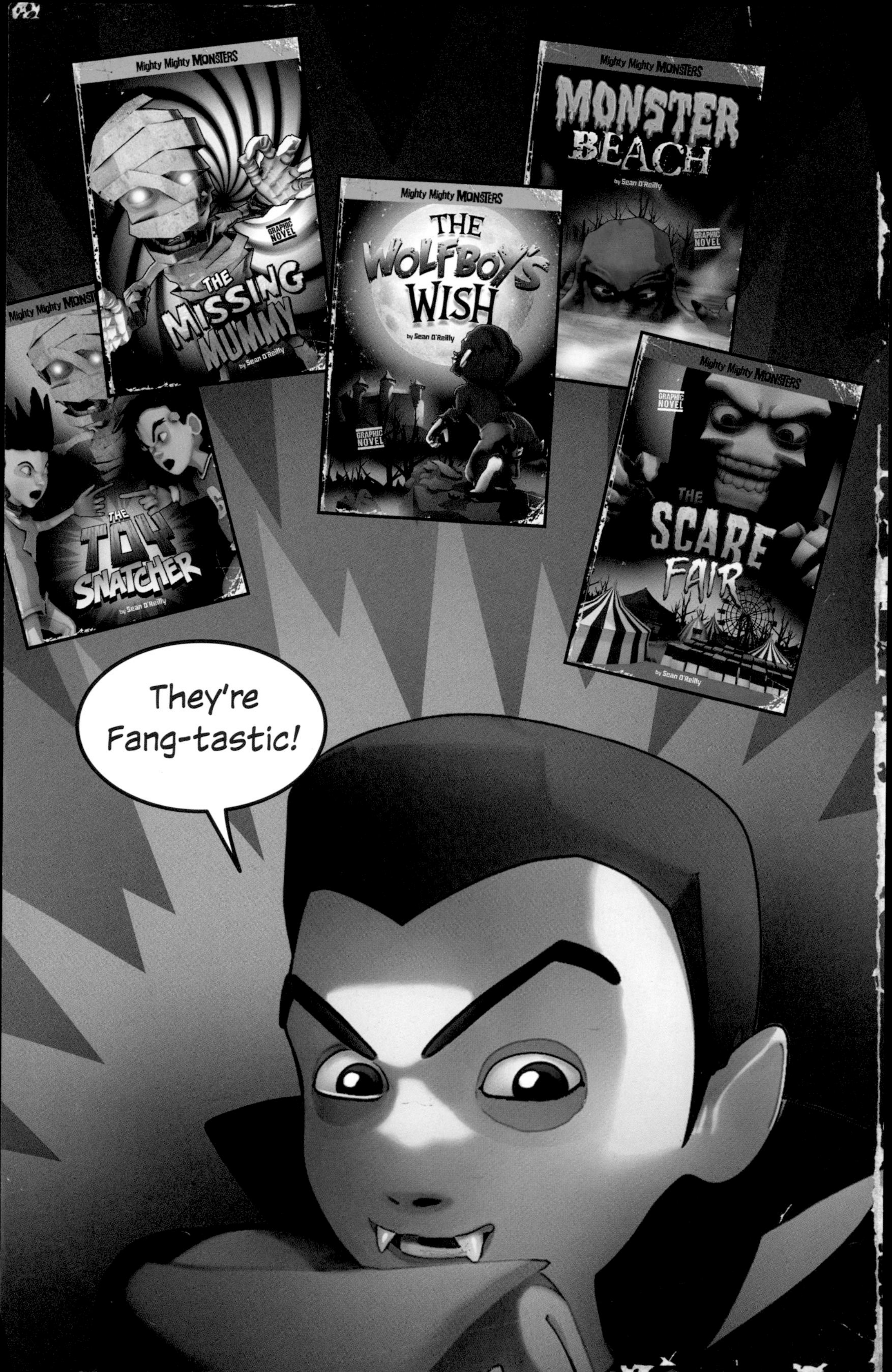
Mighty Mighty MONSTERS
THE MISSING MUMMY
by Sean O'Reilly
GRAPHIC NOVEL
Mighty Mighty MONSTERS
THE WOLFBOY'S WISH
by Sean O'Reilly
GRAPHIC NOVEL
Mighty Mighty MONSTERS
MONSTER BEACH
by Sean O'Reilly
GRAPHIC NOVEL
Mighty Mighty MONSTERS
THE TOY SNATCHER
by Sean O'Reilly
Mighty Mighty MONSTERS
GRAPHIC NOVEL
THE SCARE FAIR
by Sean O'Reilly
They're Fang-tastic!

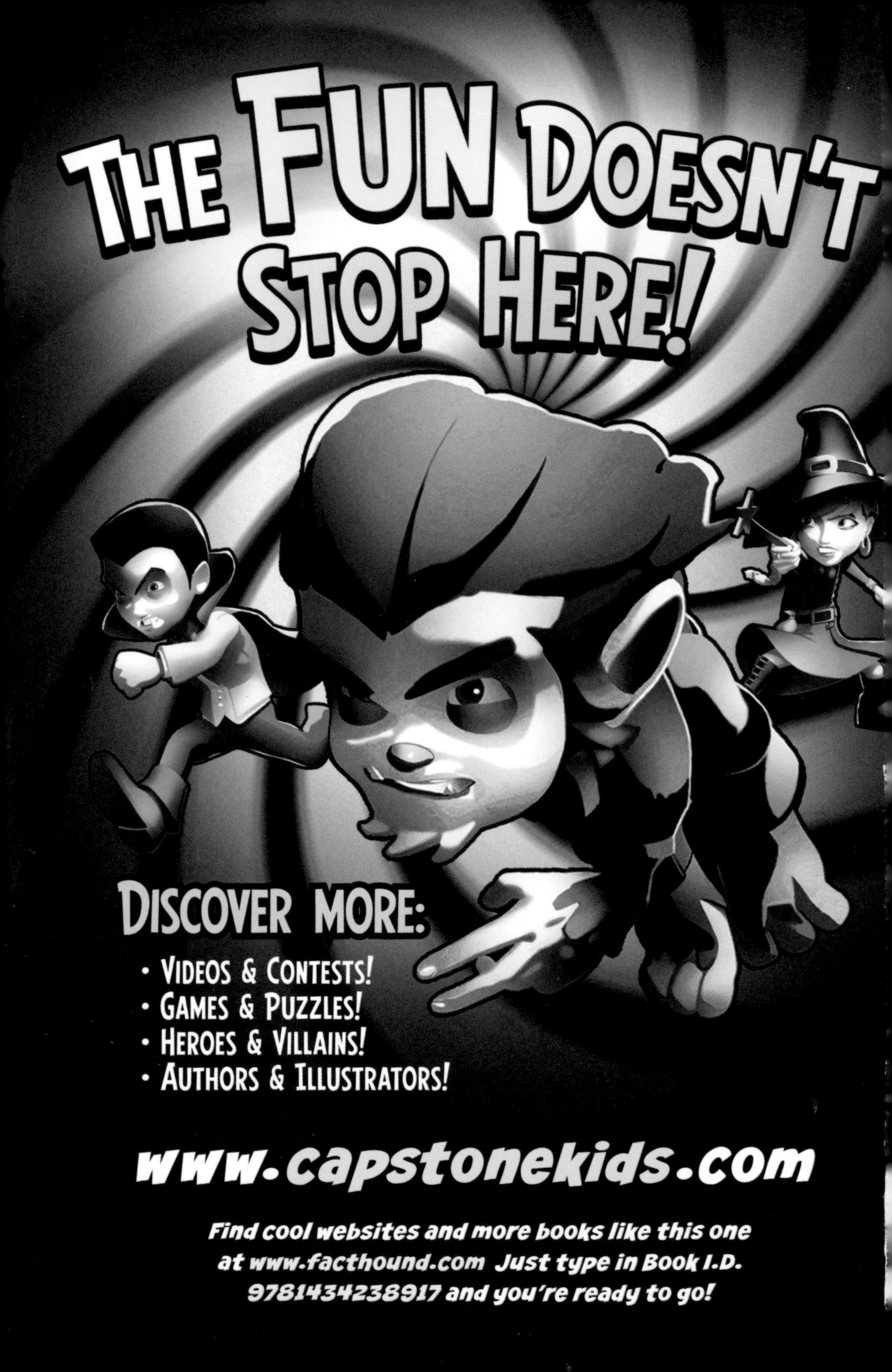
THE FUN DOESN'T STOP HERE!
DISCOVER MORE:
• VIDEOS & CONTESTS!
• GAMES & PUZZLES!
• HEROES & VILLAINS!
• AUTHORS & ILLUSTRATORS!
www.capstonekids.com
Find cool websites and more books like this one at www.facthound.com Just type in Book I.D. 9781434238917 and you're ready to go!